Buchanan's
Texas
Treasure

Buchanan's Texas Treasure

Jonas Ward

A FAWCETT GOLD MEDAL BOOK

Fawcett Publications, Inc., Greenwich, Connecticut

BUCHANAN'S TEXAS TREASURE

ISBN 0–449–13812–7

Printed in the United States of America

10 9 8 7 6 5 4 3 2 1

1

Buchanan was back in Texas. Astride the big black horse Nightshade, he had come down over rimrock to the state in which he was born with a glimmering of an idea in his romantic mind. He was six feet four and a yard wide, sandy-haired, florid of complexion, his body slightly marred by the scars of many unsought battles, but a fine figure of a man withal. His revolvers were packed in the saddlebags as always, his rifle hooded in its scabbard at his knee.

He had been up and down and around the West, caught wind of a rumor gabbled by a borracho in a Silver City bar on the high plain of New Mexico and on a whim, no more, he had come southward to check it out. He had heard the tale long ago—it was of buried treasure. Now a familiar name had been mentioned.

He came to the Cuesta property in Nueces and climbed a broken wall. This had been a fort, but it was long abandoned. He looked down at the meandering creek and the oak-lined hills beyond.

In the hills, it was thought, the treasure had been hidden during an Indian attack which had wiped out all but two of the Cuesta expedition. It was so long ago that the many diggings by treasure seekers were merely depressions in the soil where the granjeno bushes now grew. The creek widened at one point where a small dam had been built. He saw movement there and unlimbered the field glasses he had carried since he had won them from a cavalry officer in a poker game at El Paso long ago.

A girl's figure leaped into the prism of the glasses. She was in the water. She was nude. Her clothes hung neatly from a tree limb.

There was a man between her and the garments. He was a large man in tight pants and a varicolored shirt like the ones sold in the expensive shops of big cities. His hat was set on the back of his head and he was laughing. Behind the man were two cowboys, lounging on their ponies, grinning from ear to ear.

Buchanan folded away the glasses. He reached for the .44 Remington. He pointed Nightshade down the hill.

The people grew in his vision. He heard voices. The girl was not screaming. She had lowered herself into the water until only her head was in view. She was speaking quite loudly and clearly when Buchanan came silently within hearing distance. He reined in and replaced the rifle, listening with admiration—and with shock.

The girl was cursing the man and his companions. She was using deliberate West country phrasing. She seemed absolutely unafraid, so that for a moment, Buchanan had the fleeting thought that this was none of his business, possibly a lovers' spat.

Buchanan prided himself on minding his own business.

He was, above all, a peaceable man. He was about to turn Nightshade away from the slightly racy, bucolic scene when a shot rang out.

The effect was instantaneous. The three men wheeled and moved—the riders spread, reaching for weapons, and the big man who had been taunting the girl flattened himself. The girl let out a yip and swam for the edge of the pool formed by the dam.

There was a single rider coming from the south. Buchanan reached for the glasses. One glance and he hastily put them away and came riding in, not too fast.

A handsome woman was swooping down upon the scene. Her flat hat had fallen from raven locks, slightly gray at the temples. She wore Levi's and expensive tooled boots, a man's shirt, and a gun. She was shooting at the three men, but because she was seated on the back of the speeding white horse, she was not having much luck.

Buchanan called, "Molly! Molly Cuesta!"

Her voice was throaty and clear. "What are you waitin' for, you big monkey?"

"Just an invitation," he said meekly, riding at her side. "You aimin' to kill somebody?"

"I'll murder every mother's son of 'em!" She fired her last round, again without hitting anyone.

Buchanan put Nightshade in the lead, shielding Molly O'Rourke Cuesta, a friend of olden days, and rode to the brink of the limpid pool. The cowboys closed in now, sensing that the shooting was ended. The big man got to his feet and faced them, a half smile on his handsome features.

The girl in the water came halfway out into view, yelling, "Ma! Farmington's been makin' at me. Him and those other two wouldn't let me get to my duds."

Molly O'Rourke Cuesta wheeled her white pony

around, then ran it straight at the big man. He laughed, moving aside. He moved very well, Buchanan noted. The two cowhands, their composure restored, closed in on either side of Señora Cuesta.

Buchanan sighed and dismounted, trailing the reins. He strolled to where the big man was still laughing. He said, "Time to call off your hounds, there, mister."

The man named Farmington was wearing tight buckskin gloves. He swung around, backhanding, moving like a cat. He caught Buchanan by surprise. The blow had astounding authority; Buchanan went down on his haunches. The two riders brayed like mules.

It had been many a long year since anyone had knocked down Tom Buchanan. He did not enjoy the sensation. Now he saw the big man reaching for a gun worn in a spring shoulder holster. He reacted promptly, without reasoning, purely upon reflex.

He uncurled his long legs. He kicked Farmington in the exact middle. As he did so he came to his feet. Farmington shot backward into the hindquarters of the horse of one of his riders. The horse bucked, demanding all the attention of the man in the saddle.

Farmington was doubled over, swaying, still reaching for his gun. Buchanan moved in close, paused for a moment to get perfect balance, then threw an uppercut which had served him a hundred times in the past. It caught the big man in fancy clothing right on the chin.

Molly Cuesta said in her deep voice, "That's the end of the party. You, Sandy Wills . . . Don Doug James . . . don't you make a bad move!"

She had a .38 Smith & Wesson in her hand. The cowboys managed their ponies and were silent. They were now far from amused. Their eyes were narrowed beneath hat brims as they sat tanned and motionless and looked down at their fallen boss.

"Put him on his cayuse, will you, Buchanan?" the woman asked. She was backing toward the edge of the water, as though to further protect the girl.

Buchanan said, "My pleasure, Molly."

The man was a heavyweight. He was thoroughly unconscious. Buchanan placed him face down across an ornate saddle that adorned the barrel of a beautiful roan horse.

"Now get out of here. This is C-R land and you all know it," commanded the woman. "I'll take up this other dirty business with your boss later. Vamos!"

The riders had still not spoken a word. They closed in on either side of their boss. They turned southward, moving gingerly, making certain that he did not sway or tumble from his uncomfortable perch. One by one they took turns staring backward, as though to positively identify Buchanan. Then they were gone around a bend in the creek.

Molly dismounted. She stood with her hands on her hips and addressed the naked girl in the pool. "You Patricia! It's another one of your doin's. You get yourself out here and put on these clothes. And where's your blue horse?"

"Those dirty varmints ran him off," cried the girl. "That damn Hal Farmington wouldn't let me get to my clothes."

She swam three vigorous strokes and stood up. The water was barely to her knees. Buchanan, taken once more by surprise, spun around, turning his back.

Molly O'Rourke Cuesta said to him, "You see her?"

"Well, I didn't have a mind to stare," he replied. He was beginning to feel a bit abused. His face ached from the whopping blow which had downed him. "Your daughter, no doubt."

"Course she's my daughter. Would I come roarin' down here shootin' if she wasn't?"

Buchanan observed, "She sure favors you a lot. I mind when you were young. Always swimmin' in a creek or a pond or wherever."

"And once in the Pacific Ocean." For the first time the woman smiled. There were lines at the corners of her wide mouth and tiny crows feet adorning each blue eye, but she was as vital as the Texas springtime. "How've you been, anyway, Buchanan?"

"Just fine," he said. "How's the señor?"

The handsome face clouded. "He ain't with us any more."

"No!"

"He went looking for the treasure again. The last time. They dry-gulched him." Her voice was grim and cold. "Never could find the tracks, couldn't find anything. But someone knew he was onto something. And they got him and Enriquez and Donovan."

Buchanan said, "I sure am sorry. Benito was *muy hombre*."

The vitality drained from the woman. "He was that."

Buchanan had known them when the girl Patricia Ann was a baby. They were ten or a dozen years older than he but it had not made any difference as they saw the elephant together in San Francisco, doing the theaters, the Barbary Coast, the beaches. Molly had been the best swimmer of them all. It had been a wonderful time.

The girl came around and into his line of vision. She was tall, like her mother, dark like her father. She must be about seventeen, he thought. She wore a loose shirt and a pair of men's pants and low-cut boots. Her hair was pulled back, soaking wet, tied with a limp ribbon. She was as beautiful as a sunset on the mountains.

Molly said, "Patricia Ann, this is Tom Buchanan. Best we get back to the house. I don't trust Hal Farmington from here to there."

"He won't kill anyone," the girl said. "He just wants me to marry him, that's all."

"It's enough." Molly's voice regained its timbre. "I'm not sure yet that he didn't murder your father."

"Oh, hell," said the girl dismissing the notion as either absurd or unimportant. "Who am I going to ride with, you or this Buchanan fella?"

"You're going to ride with me," her mother told her. "I've got troubles enough without you getting ideas about Tom."

The girl grinned, then winked. She seemed entirely unaffected by the violence of the previous scene. She said to Buchanan, "Molly's turned out to be a papa and a woman rolled into one. Gee, Hal sure did knock you on your behind now, didn't he?"

"He sure did," Buchanan admitted. "He's got a real good backhand."

The girl leaped aboard her mother's white horse in one lithe move. "He won't be satisfied 'til he's tried it again. You kicked him before you knocked him out. He'll make that his excuse."

"I can't wait for his next excuse," said Buchanan. "I'm a peaceable man but fisticuffs ain't really what I call violence. When you see him again, tell him I'll be around."

They headed in the direction from which Molly O'Rourke Cuesta had ridden. There was brush and the trail wandered. There was no rhythm to the land after they left the waterway. There were a few steers here and

there, munching the stark herbage. They weren't fat
enough for the spring drive; Buchanan frowned at them.

This was country neither utterly strange nor very familiar to him. He had ridden brush but he had never
visited the old Cuesta ranch. Time and tide had taken
him elsewhere throughout the Western country. It was the
rumor of the treasure and his remembrance of Benito and
Molly as good companions that had brought him here,
more or less without definite aim. He never craved gold;
he had enough for his small needs. He was a man of the
outdoors, and he would rather fish and hunt and con-
template nature than spend his time in towns. Above all,
however, he cherished friends.

When they came to the old hacienda he was shocked.
The roof sagged. The fences were leaning, one way or the
other. Barbed wire had come to Texas but there was no
line of it in sight. The stable was tacky. Paint was needed
everywhere. Only the fact that the house was a hundred
years old and built honestly held it all together, he
thought.

The best men had gone down with Benito, according
to Molly, the segundo and an old retainer. He looked at
two hired hands in the corral. They seemed indolent but
the horses looked sound and he recognized a blue among
them. The older of the men came to the rails, hung a boot,
grinned and addressed Molly Cuesta.

"See you found her okay, ma'am. Swimmin' again?"

He was near middle age, bowlegged, mahogany-faced,
squinting eyes. About him was an air of not quite belonging, yet he bore a note of authority.

Molly said, "My foreman, Bottles Jimson. The other
one is the wrangler, Pecos Harder." She pointed at Jimson. "How come you didn't go huntin' her when Blue
came home without her?"

"Shoot, ma'am, it happens all the time. Patricia don't tie him down."

"He'll stand if I tell him to, you ninny," yipped the girl. "He was run off by those damn Farmingtons."

"Sorry about that." Jimson didn't seem concerned. "You need us for anything?"

Buchanan said, "My hoss, here, Nightshade. He needs some oats and some attendin' to. You mind if I go right on ahead?"

Molly said, "The name's Buchanan. Tom Buchanan. He's my guest."

Bottles Jimson surveyed the powerful, huge black with respect. "Yes, sir. Hoss like that, he deserves special 'tention."

"If you'll excuse me, Molly?" Buchanan rode to the barn. He watched out of the corner of his eye as the two women dismounted and walked toward the house. It seemed to him that the foreman and the silent, lanky man exchanged sly glances and secret smiles. He led Nightshade to a stall, removed the saddle and gear, and found straw with which to rub him down. There were oats in a bin, not of the first grade. He shook down straw for bedding and forked hay into the manger. Then he took his rifle and his saddlebags and went to the rear door of the ranch house. He had a growing bad feeling about the setup at this ranch, which had been in the Cuesta family since before Texas had joined the Union.

Further, Molly had mentioned only a couple of hands who were out on the roundup. It was coming time for the spring drive—yet the foreman and an extra man were fiddling around in the home corral. It was all wrong.

2

Hal Farmington returned to consciousness. The two riders had paused by the edge of the stream, safely out of reach or view of Buchanan and the two women. They had placed him against the trunk of an oak tree and were gently administering to him.

Sandy Wills, red-haired, bolder than his companion, said, "Didn't want to take you home until you was okay, Hal."

Don Doug James, bigger, a solid man, nodded and fanned Farmington with his sombrero. The horses nibbled at the rough vegetation. It could have been a nice warm day in Nueces County but it was not.

Farmington asked feebly, "Did you get his name?"

"Buchanan," said Sandy Wills. "Name of Buchanan. Heard of him aplenty. You sure cold-cocked him, Hal."

"Cold-cock him I did not," muttered Farmington. He touched his jaw. "Does it show?"

"Not much," said the cowboy.

"Will the old man be able to tell?"

"Not if you keep your chin in and your collar up."

Farmington said, "The bastard kicked me."

"He sure did."

"I could whip him in a fair fight."

"Never did see the man you couldn't beat." But Sandy looked sideways at Don Doug James, who lifted a shoulder ever so slightly. "Thing is, this Buchanan's been travelin' with a black champion name of Coco Bean. He sent Bean back East to fight the best they got."

"Eastern boxers will whip anyone from the West," Farmington said. He was regaining his voice along with some composure.

"Never been East myself," said Sandy cheerfully. "Anyways, this Buchanan, he's some part of a fighter his own self, they do say."

"We'll see about that." Farmington's head went up. "I'll look him up as soon as possible."

"Whatever you say, Hal." The cowhands waited respectfully for the next move.

Farmington arose, steadied himself against the tree for a moment, then demanded, "Where were you two while all this was happening to me?"

"Under Señora Cuesta's gun," said Sandy, shrugging.

"A woman held the two of you back?"

"You want us to shoot the señora?"

Farmington said, "No, of course not. But you might have tried something."

"Nothin' we could think of," Sandy said. "You want to go back home, now? We got to pop that brush and round up somethin' for Box F."

"Yes. We'll go home now."

He always carried himself proudly but his innards were

boiling now, remembering Buchanan's boots into his mid-riff, the swiftness and power of Buchanan's wallop to the chin. That it should be witnessed by Patricia Cuesta was bad enough, but that both women had seen it—and enjoyed it—was a blow from which he could never recover until he had his revenge.

He rode for the home ranch. The house was two-storied, gable-roofed with dormer windows. His father had built it just a few years ago, when the Farmingtons had moved westward as their Wall Street fortune dwindled during the panic. His father had never wanted to make the move, had no interest in cattle raising. Only the continuing rumor about the Cuesta buried treasure had kept old Judson Farmington interested, in fact.

Hal Farmington had been the child of middle age. His mother had died giving birth to him. His father was now into his seventies, a tyrant oblivious to past failures, a self-styled king of the Box F acreage, the biggest spread in the county. Hal Farmington did as he was told for the most part. He did not like it; he had cultivated the respect of Sandy and Don Doug so that he might use them when he needed help.

One thing he did like—his father had commanded him to court Patricia Ann Cuesta. That is, he liked the thought that one day she might succumb. Up until now it had been no pleasure. She had rejected him a dozen times.

Yet she had smiled, until today. He had made a mistake by keeping her in the water, threatening her. He realized it now. He would never admit it to anyone else, especially his father, but it had been a tactical error.

He could trust Sandy and Wills, he believed. Actually all the Box F men were together because there was a goal. They wanted to put together a herd for the trail north—and they all thirsted for the treasure of the Cuesta family.

Hal Farmington turned over his horse to the men and went into the house that so resembled the one in which he had been born back in Boston. His father was, as usual, in the library, a book-lined room at the east side of the building.

The old man was wiry, strong as a goat, with a goat's beard and eyes. His hands were never still as he sat behind his desk and played with ancient documents.

"Don't tell me," he said. "You had no luck with the Cuesta bitch."

"If they hear you calling her a bitch there will be real trouble," said Hal. "They don't talk like that out here."

"What do I care how they talk?" demanded the old man. "What do I care about half-breed women? The Cuestas never married beneath themselves until that generation, Benito's generation. I have here the whole history."

"Yes, father, I know." But he also knew he would have to listen. He sat in a stuffed chair, in the shadow lest his father detect the bruise given him by Buchanan.

"They had a fortune in gold bullion. They had silver plate worth thousands back East in today's mart. They had jewels beyond price." Judson Farmington's eyes gleamed, his voice reverberated in the high-ceilinged room. "They were favorites of the king's governors. And they were attacked by savages."

"It was a hundred years ago," muttered Hal Farmington.

"They fought. They got away from the house and tried to reach New Mexico. They failed. Somewhere along the line they buried that treasure." He waved a crackling parchment, brown at the edges. "One of them survived, maybe two. They got to Santa Fe. It is all here, put down in their own language. This is the second time I have discovered a document which relates the identical story."

"But no map," said his son.

"Of course no map. It was intended that it be told by word of mouth. Something interposed." He jumped up from the chair and moved from behind the desk, striding up and down the Oriental rug he had brought from Boston. "If we could only find the key to what happened. Why didn't Benito know the exact location of the hiding place?"

"You never let him get there," said Hal.

"It was accidental," said his father sternly. "The entire matter was accidental."

"They saw you first."

"They suspected an ambush by Indians just as it had happened to Benito's ancestors. Thus, they fired upon us as we followed them."

"And you wiped them out. They might have been able to answer some questions if they'd lived." Hal's voice was low; he had buried his chin in his collar.

The father whirled. "Are you criticizing me and my men? Are you suggesting we could have acted in any other manner?"

"No. It's all over, no use to even talk about it," said Hal. "I apologize."

"And well you should! I send you to Harvard, a big, strapping fellow with good looks inherited from me. You fail. I bring you out here and ask you to court a half-savage girl whose language is that of a common street-walker. You fail. I will brook no criticism from you, young man."

The son fought back choler. A thousand times he had done this when his father adopted a certain tone. No matter how often he tried to refrain from argument, it always came to the point where he became furious. He said throatily, "I admit I do not have your charm, Father. I already have apologized for any implied criticism. I must point out, however, that if we do not make a herd to go up the trail we will inevitably be very short of cash."

"You think I'm not aware of that?" The older man bristled. "Make your herd. But above all, remember this: It is the Cuesta treasure which will restore us and return us to the East where we belong!"

Hal Farmington sighed. "Yes, Father."

"Move in on that woman! You have your two chosen partners. Do something!"

He was tempted to say that he had tried something this very afternoon. But he could not confide in his father, a lesson he had learned long ago. Any admissions of defeat would be held against him. And if he revealed the fact that he would give up the treasure to possess the alluring Patricia. . . . He coughed and said, "Uh—I think Señora Cuesta has brought in a gunman."

"Is that so? And why have you practiced the draw all those hours? You mean you can't cope with a gunman?"

"I didn't say that. I only . . ."

"I don't care a continental hoot what Señora Cuesta does excepting that she does not locate that treasure before I get my hands on it." Judson Farmington's voice rang like a bell. "Now you go and do what you must about the cattle. I'll concentrate and try to do the thinking around here."

"Yes, sir," said the son. He walked out of the room. It was absolutely amazing the effect his father had upon him. He squirmed inwardly when in the same room with the old fellow. He was simply, flatly scared of him.

He was not scared of anything else, he told himself. He

had knocked the big man down. . . . He felt his jaw where it hurt. If it were not for Molly Cuesta's gun and the presence of the girl he coveted he would have resumed the fight. He knew every trick of the game; he had trained with champions. He had never met the man he could not whip by fair means or foul.

Including his father . . .

Buchanan ladled up the last of the chile. His mouth and throat burned with the pleasure all Texans derived from the Mexican dish. He sighed with pleasure.

"Molly, you're still the champion. Long time since I've had such a scrumptious meal."

"Have some more?"

"Couldn't manage it. Three helpin's is more'n a sober man should help himself to."

She smiled at him. "Consuela made apple pie this mornin'. Reckon you can handle a piece."

"Now that's different. Comes to the end of a feed the appetite revives itself for apple pie."

They were eating in the dining room, after the fashion of the Spanish-American ranchers. Bottles Jimson and Pecos were in the kitchen, exchanging poor jokes with the young Consuela, who helped Molly with the cooking and other household tasks.

Patricia Ann said, "No pie for me. I'm going to look after Blue. If y'all will excuse me."

She strode out. She was a strong filly, Buchanan thought, and probably needed gentling. She was not a great talker but her eyes flashed as she listened to her elders. She had, he thought, private misgivings.

Molly Cuesta stared across the table. "Tom, I couldn't do anything but level with you. Things are bad. Damn bad."

"Hard thing for a woman to run a ranch."

"Hardest thing is to get help. Good men seem to hate workin' for a woman. And then there's the damn treasure."

"You mean everyone's still looking for that bundle of gold and jewels that may not ever have existed?"

She was silent for a moment. Then she said, "It's in existence. It's somewhere around here."

"How can you be sure?" asked Buchanan. "A hundred years is a whale of a long time."

"Even Bottles thinks he knows something. Him and his sidekick, Pecos, always hangin' around."

"I wondered. They oughta be out chousin' cattle."

"I've tried to send them. Bottles always has an excuse. You know how it is. Benito was the boss. I'm just not used to it."

Louder laughter came from the kitchen. Molly flushed and bit her lip. She started to rise, then sat down and murmured, "If I yell on them they'll prob'ly quit."

Buchanan asked, "You want me to get into it?"

"I can't hire any more men," Molly said in a low voice. "I just can't pay."

After a moment he said, "I don't hire out, truth to tell. But what with one thing and another, some jobs just come flat up and take over. You want them outa here tonight?"

"I do."

He said, "Then I'm hired. I'm the new segundo. I work for Molly Cuesta. Right?"

"Right," she said, relief flooding her voice. She went on, "Tom, I know how you are. You ain't crazy about money and things. But I got to warn you, everybody else around here is. And that treasure is on everybody's mind."

"Cattle's your business and it don't look too good. I

can check it out," he told her. "Now we better talk to
Jimson."

"He and Pecos," she agreed. "They're kinda slick. And
Pecos is sneaky quick. I don't know what they're up to
but they worry me."

"Uh-huh." Buchanan followed her into the spacious
kitchen, with its huge stove, long trestle table, benches,
zinc sink, pump handle for water, shelves for crockery,
a door open to the pantry. The Mexican girl was against the
far wall, laughingly protesting as the two men teased her.

Molly said, "Consuela."

The girl made a swift, darting move and came to where
the mistress of Cuesta Ranch stood, with legs slightly
spread, hands on hips.

"Si, señora."

"Clear the table."

"Si, señora." The girl vanished.

Molly said, "Bottles. Pecos. Meet your new boss."

The faces of the two men changed, became contorted
with amazement, then went blank. Bottles was the first to
speak, as always.

"Didn't think the shebang could afford another hand,"
said he.

Buchanan said, "Don't let it worry your head. Best you
get your gear together and head out for the roundup."

Jimson cocked his head to one side and addressed
Molly. "You reckon?"

"I reckon," she told him.

"There ain't enough C-R beef out there to make a
drive. You know it."

"Then why am I hiring you?" she demanded.

"What there is, Farmington's bunch will be chousin' it
around to all corners."

Buchanan asked, "Are you scared of Farmington and his men?"

Jimson lost his sly look for a moment, eyeing Buchanan, his eyes narrowed to catlike slits. "Mr. Buchanan, I personal ain't scared of nobody nohow. You're a mighty big fella. I ain't scared of you."

"Then why don't you go ahead and do what's asked of you?" asked Buchanan without raising his voice. "Seems like the foreman and the wrangler should be where they're needed."

Pecos was already moving toward the door. Jimson slowly joined him, then turned and said, "Molly, I hope this hombre is okay. Reason we didn't go before, we hated to leave you women here alone. Farmington's made some threats on you."

"Tom Buchanan knocked Hal Farmington into a cocked hat this afternoon while you were hanging around here," Molly said sharply. "Now will you get goin'?"

Bottles Jimson again surveyed Buchanan, shaking his head. "Nobody beats on a Farmington nor none of their people without trouble upcomin'. Keep your eyes peeled, Buchanan. They'll be comin' for you."

"I'm a peaceable man," Buchanan replied. "But when they come, I'll be waitin'."

The two men slid out of the door. They did not move with the rolling gait of cowboys long accustomed to the saddle. Buchanan wanted to ask questions about them but Molly was distraught and he followed her back into the dining room, through a parlor laden with heavy Spanish furniture, and into a room that had obviously been the office of Benito Cuesta. There was a big, carved desk, several deep chairs whose leather was beginning to crack, and in the corner a huge iron safe. Molly sat be-

hind the desk. She looked small and worn, older than her
true age.

Buchanan dropped into one of the chairs and asked,
"Jimson said Farmingtons. More'n one?"

"Two, father and son. The old man is a bastard of the
first order. Came here from Boston with cash and bought
everything surrounding us."

"But you wouldn't sell."

"I promised Benito."

"On account of the Cuesta treasure."

"Yes. Benito believed in the treasure."

"Inca gold and jewels, the way they tell it."

"They do indeed. Brought up to the old original Cuesta
a hundred years ago for safekeeping. And then the Indians attacked. And they tried to get away and they
couldn't get far enough ahead. So they hid the treasure—
buried it somewhere. Then they were all killed except
maybe there was one or two got away." She spread her
hands on the desk. "I do believe part of it. I have to
believe."

"People have searched. On and off your property."

"Plenty of them—and found nothing."

Buchanan said, "To my thinkin' it would be impossible
to dig a big enough hole deep enough in the time they had
before the Indians got to them."

"I know." She sighed. "And of course we know not a
hunk of it ever showed up. Not when the Apaches were
in their wars. Not in Mexico. Not anyplace."

Buchanan said, "Molly, in a hundred years the land
shifts. There are earthquakes, floods. Rivers change
courses. Where could they have buried the treasure?"

"That's what I don't know," she confessed. "But I
found the parchment."

"The parchment?" Buchanan sat up straight. "You mean somethin' a hundred years old?"

"Yes. Benito had it hidden in a ledger stuffed 'way in the back of the safe." She pointed to the huge iron box.

"You got it now?"

"It's in there, where he put it. Farmington's sent people to steal it. They never got near it."

"How does Farmington know about it?"

"Somethin' he learned back East. From a library or someplace. Don't ask me how it got out, unless somebody escaped the Indians. You know plenty of those old Spaniards walked across country at different times in different places. And they told tall tales."

"That's true." Buchanan found himself suddenly interested.

"And the damn parchment is incomplete," she said. "Maybe the one who got away took part of it with him."

"They must've been in a big hurry," Buchanan agreed. "Anything like that could've happened."

"It's the only thing I can figure." She shook her head. "What I've got don't tell where they buried it, that's for sure. It's tormented me since I found it."

The young voice of Patricia Ann Cuesta interrupted from the doorway. "Ma, you're not going to show it to a stranger!"

Molly straightened in the chair behind the desk. "Did I ask your advice, Patricia Ann?"

"You don't need to," said the girl coldly. "I say nobody gets to look at it."

"And I say we need a man to help." She looked pleadingly at Buchanan. "You'll give your word not to tell anyone what it is, won't you?"

"Uh-huh," said Buchanan, shrugging. He stared at the

tall girl. "Not that I'm used to bein' questioned in matters of this kind."

"I question any stranger, man, woman or child," said the girl harshly. "It means too damn much to us. It means our lives. You know what happens to women with nothin', no money, no land, no home."

"Uh-huh," repeated Buchanan. "Thing is, you haven't got it now. You need to find it. You got people tryin' to get to it before you do. Nobody's goin' to share with y'all."

Patricia Ann challenged, "And what about you? What would be your share?"

"Well lemme see," Buchanan ruminated. "Time? That's all I got is time and it's worth nothin'. Gold? I don't actually need any, it's bulky and it don't buy anything I want. Maybe—let's see—a pretty jewel for a friend?"

"A girl friend, I suppose."

Buchanan shook his head. "A mother of as fine a baby as you ever saw. Her husband's like my adopted son."

"Fine story!" She strode to the desk and leaned over so that her face was close to her mother. "I say we don't trust him. I say we keep lookin' on our own."

Molly Cuesta shook her head. "You're just like your father. You've got a Latin head. I say Tom Buchanan was sent by Providence."

Patricia Ann cried, "I won't let you do it!" and ran to the safe. She stood in front of it, her arms spread. Her bosom was upthrust, her eyes darted fire.

Molly sighed. "Tom?"

"Anything I hate is to bust into a family argument. Still, when someone's bein' plumb obstinate. . . ." He came out of the chair like a grizzly bear. He put his huge hands beneath the arms of the tall girl, lifted her, and swung her around and away from the safe.

She flailed at him. She did not scream; she saved her

breath. She connected with the sore spot where Farmington had landed.

Buchanan shifted his grip. In a jiffy he had her turned sideways, limbs flailing. He sat down on a straight backed hardwood and rawhide chair. He whipped the big girl down over his knees. He grinned at Molly and said, "Go ahead, if you want to. Open the safe. Or don't. Whichever, this handful won't bother you."

Suddenly Patricia Ann stopped struggling. She went limp, doubled over, the seat of her jeans pulled tight. She wept softly, wearily, her hands covering her face.

Buchanan straightened her up. He held her without force. She leaned her head against his flannel shirt and continued her silent weeping.

Molly went to the safe. She turned to look at her daughter. Her face softened. She knelt down and began to manipulate the dial. The clicking of the tumblers sounded loud in the silence.

Buchanan glanced around the room. The girl was still now, limp in his arms. There was a rifle hanging on one wall, above an Indian rug of gay colors. There were heavy drapes at the windows, which were closed. Yet there was a noise other than the whirling of the dial.

Buchanan put the girl gently on the floor at his feet. He shook his head at her, motioning for silence. He reached one long arm for the rifle, made sure that it was loaded as was the custom of the times. He tiptoed out of the office and through the dining room. He went to the kitchen where Consuela was washing dishes in a pan full of soapy water.

He whispered, "Did you hear anyone outside?"

She shook her head, her dark eyes widening. Buchanan went to the door. He waited a moment, then flung it open.

There was a stuttering of feet around on the side of the

house. He ran lightly, swiftly, levering a cartridge into the chamber of the rifle. A horse whinnied.

Two men ran and made flying leaps into the saddles of two tall, rangy mustangs. They ducked their heads and rode into the night. There was no moon and the stars were far away and hidden by fleecy clouds.

Buchanan fired with care. He had no desire to shoot a stranger in the back. He did mean to send a warning, a threat to prowlers.

One of the men fired back. Buchanan laid a bullet so close to him that he yelled and spurred his horse.

By now the girl was beside him. She carried her mother's S&W revolver. She was staring into the night.

"Farmington's men," she said. "You see? Nothing will work for us. Nothing! There's a curse on the house."

"Don't talk like that." Buchanan rebuked her. "Never believe in curses nor bad luck nor anything of the kind. And I don't know if it was Farmington's people or your own pair."

"Bottles and Pecos? They wouldn't dare."

"Maybe. Maybe not."

"It wasn't them," she said positively. "I'd know our horses."

"Uh-huh."

They went toward the house. She said, "I know horses and I know how to swim better'n anybody in this country. Believe me. I may not know much else but I know when I'm beat. And you can beat me."

"You got a gun in your hand," said Buchanan. "You could shoot me."

"You'd take it away before I got in one shot," she said. She was grinning. The light from the kitchen struck across her face and she was beautiful. "Nope. Swimmin' and horses. Those are my things."

He said, "Let me tell you, girl. If there's a way to find that treasure, it's all yours and Molly's. You got to believe me."

"I do," she said. "Now I believe you. The way you handled me, not hurtin'—nor nothin'. She says you're a good man. I got to believe."

They went into the house. They walked past the pale, frightened Consuela. Molly was behind the desk again. She had a piece of crisp, heavy parchment before her, and was studying it with a large magnifying glass. She looked up at them.

"They're always sneakin' around. Did you wing one of them, Tom?"

"No. Didn't try. Maybe taught 'em to be more careful. Buried treasure attracts 'em like flies around a honey pot. Always did, always will."

She offered him the glass. "This is what I have. Do you read Spanish?"

"Not good enough," he said.

"I'll translate it for you."

"Uh-huh." He was examining the parchment under the glass. It could be a hundred years old, he thought. It could be a humbug. The lettering was faint but decipherable, probably done with a stylus, in great haste. It was brief.

The parchment had not been torn, he thought. It had been cut with a very sharp knife. It had been sliced vertically, down the middle of the lettering, so that there were no complete sentences.

Molly began to read,

"Only God can . . .

The gold and jew . . .

But for us poor . . .

Little hope. Whoever . . .

Look for water. . . ."

She stopped and shook her head. "They didn't have much time, of course."

"That's the whole of it?" asked Buchanan.

"That's it."

"Uh-huh. It's somethin'. 'Gold and jew . . .' That's plain, gold and jewels. And there's that about water." He grinned at Patricia Ann. "So that's why you're such a great swimmer. You been lookin' into the depths."

She nodded.

Buchanan asked, "Without no clothes on?"

She stared back at him. "I have my bathing costume. I don't always wear it."

"No offense," he assured her. "What little I saw, it was about as good as one can get."

She shrugged one shoulder. "I'm not one to get that upset. Anyway, I saw you turn your back."

Molly interjected, "I've warned her a thousand times that Farmington or his men will catch her stark. It had to happen. If Farmington was mad enough . . ."

"He was mad enough," said the girl. "I told him aplenty. I told him to never speak to me again as long as he lived."

Buchanan said mildly, "It didn't appear he was the kind to let that stop him."

Molly said, "It's his father. Judson. He's determined to get the ranch. He believes the treasure must be buried on this land someplace."

"Because my papa was always looking, trying to figure it out," said Patricia Ann. She looked at Buchanan again. "You think Papa didn't know about riverbeds and all? He was tryin' to figure just which way the river bent. Or if the treasure was buried in a creek. And if the creek had dried up, then it was under brush, sand or just plain dirt. Which is what this country is made of."

"In a hundred years it could be under the roots of a mighty big tree," Buchanan added. "What we've got here is a puzzle that might never be solved."

There was silence for a while. Buchanan searched out a cleaning rod from a chest and went to work on the borrowed rifle, his mind revolving. The girl was lonely, the woman was worried. There was no way he could leave them. Yet, on the other hand, it was a hopeless venture.

Finally Molly asked in a low, inquiring voice, "Tom?"

"Uh-huh."

"Did you say 'we,' Tom?"

The eyes of both women were upon his tanned, scarred face as he worked with sure hands. He sighed.

"Benito was a hiyu man. You two—left here without him, it ain't right. Yeah, reckon that's the way it has to be. Us."

The woman and the girl descended upon him, hugging and kissing. He put down the gun and the cleaning rod, to enjoy it while it lasted.

He had broken off a bigger hunk than he could chew. But as of this moment it was certainly worth the effort.

3

Buchanan opened his eyes before dawn. He could barely make out the high ceiling of the guest room of the C-R ranch. He padded, naked, to the washbasin, and washed with great care. He was donning his inevitable long johns when the first light peered through a large window. It was cool this morning; a soft breeze spun through the room and struck him. He felt wide awake. The scars on his body ached only a little. He scratched a deep arrow wound and yawned. Then he was truly wide awake.

Now he could see the room in which he had slept. The bed was canopied, but the silken material was threadbare. There were cracks in the plaster. It was scrupulously clean and neat but the signs of poverty were in every nook and cranny.

A woman could run a ranch, he knew through experience. Some ran them better than some men. But without cash, with the cattle scattered in the brush, with inefficient help, the Cuestas could do little. He gazed down upon a vegetable garden that was doing a lot better than the rest of the shebang. Consuela was picking here and there, gathering greens and potatoes and corn from a small stand. She was a pretty girl, a bit heavy in the hips but lithe.

Buchanan pulled on his working pants and donned a checkered wool shirt. He struggled into worn but serviceable boots.

He hesitated a long moment, then removed from his saddlebags a Colt .44, which was wrapped in chamois. He wiped oil from it with a rag, spun the cylinders from long habit. He loaded five cylinders, made sure his belt was full of bullets, slung it over his shoulder. He hated to carry a short gun but he was in dangerous country and a man was a fool not to be ready for trouble if trouble came along.

He trailed his .44 Remington and went down the stairs, which were worn and a bit rickety. It would take a lot of money to restore the C-R to the mansion of the brush country it had been.

He went to the kitchen and there was the odor of ham and eggs and pancakes and molasses. He said, "Well, you're up beforetimes for a young gal."

Patricia Ann was flushed by the heat of the stove. Her color deepened as she replied. "If there's a man in the house, he should be took care of."

"Now that's a sentiment which I like a heap," he told her. He hung up the gunbelt, his hat, propped the rifle in the corner below the wooden pegs arranged in a line. He rubbed his sandy hair and sat down at the long table. "No hands to feed this mornin'?"

"Those lazy waddies are out where they belong, thanks

to you," said the girl. She looked fresh and restored, as though the night's sleep and what had gone before bedtime had worked a spell upon her.

"Mama sleeps late?" He grinned at her.

She lost the brilliance for a moment. "Mama can fight. But it wearies her. I think she's not as strong as she was."

"Something wrong?"

"I don't know." Consuela came in with an apron full of garden produce and Patricia Ann shut her mouth tight and began heaping hot cakes, eggs and bacon on a huge platter. "She told me that you eat a heap."

"One of life's real pleasures," acknowledged Buchanan.

"Big as you are, it takes a lot of fodder to keep you goin'." She flashed him an admiring glance, her spirits restored. "You goin' out today?"

"I aim to look around."

"Right." She sat down opposite him, allowing Consuela to take over. The girl put another heaping plate before her and Patricia Ann attacked it.

In a moment Consuela had fixed herself a smaller portion of food and seated herself at the end of the table. Buchanan regarded her closely for a moment, then spoke to her.

"Ramon Rodriguez was your father?"

"*Sí*," she said, startled.

"You were a yearling when I was here last."

"*Sí*, señor."

Patricia Ann said, "You got some memory. She was a skinny little brat when you saw her last."

"My father died with Señor Cuesta," the girl said proudly. "Murdered. By the Farmingtons, no?"

"We got no proof," Patricia Ann said. "All we know is that the Farmingtons were lookin' for the treasure same time as Papa went out with his men."

"You reckon young Farmington's a killer, Patricia Ann?"

"No. But his old man, now. He'd kill a baby to get his own way. The son's scared pea beans of him."

Buchanan thought for a moment. "When your pa went out last time, you think he had a good notion where to look?"

"Ma thought so. He talked about it so much she got tired of listening. So the last time he didn't say."

"What do you think?"

"I don't know. But Farmington's got somethin' or other, like we said. They came out here with maps and such. I got that from Hal; he talks a lot with his mouth."

"And he's scared of his old man."

"And he wants to marry me. Huh!"

"He's not scared of a fight."

"No, he ain't. You look out for him."

Buchanan swallowed a mouthful of food. "He was quick with that sneak punch."

"He's gun quick, too," she said, frowning. "Carries it under his arm like a town gambler. I seen him draw. . . . He was showin' off."

"I noticed the gun. Met people like him before now."

"I heard tell. Ma and Pa talked about you and your times and things."

"Your pa was a good man. We had high old fun together, the three of us."

"And your lady friends."

Buchanan shrugged. "Those were good times."

"There ain't been any good times here since Pa was killed."

Buchanan stopped eating. In her voice had been the despair of the young to whom tragedy is very near. He said quietly, "You think about good times comin' back."

"I just can't. Not yet." She stood up, pulling back her long hair, twisting it into a braid. "I'll ride with you. It'll help."

"I aim to pop some brush this mornin'."

"What do you think I been doin'? Before I took that swim I was in the brush."

He said, "In them clothes?"

"No. And we got leggins for you, big as you are. And maybe a jacket. You know the brush?"

"I know it." He hesitated. "What about your ma and the girl, here?"

"They both can shoot. They been alone a heap." She started for the door. "Then there's Rafe."

"Rafe?"

"He didn't ride with Pa and them. He never got over it, I reckon. But he does chores. He'll be in the bunkhouse."

"He on the payroll?"

"He works for room and grub. Ma—she's sorry for him."

"But you're not?"

"Oh, I reckon. Would you be?"

"Accordin' to whether he stayed home because he was scared—or crooked—or whatever."

"He . . . well, he's lame," she said.

Buchanan thought about that. "Better get goin'," he said.

"I'm ready." She clapped a soft felt hat on her head, covering the braids. She wore Levi's and well-worn boots. She walked like a horsewoman, a slightly rolling gait— but she was not, he noted, bowlegged.

They went to the stable and Nightshade whinnied, preening, already curried, combed and saddled. An old man led forth the roan known as Blue.

Patricia Ann said, "You been at it mighty early Rafe. This here is Tom Buchanan, the new boss."

The figure limped forward as with reluctance, looking up at Buchanan. "Howdy."

Buchanan snapped his fingers. "Rafe Connors. That's it. I couldn't remember, there, for a minute."

"It's what is left of me," said Rafe.

"Uh-huh. Way I heard it, you got hurt down in Chihuahua some years back."

"You heard right." He was a gaunt figure, gray-bearded. He had eyes of faded blue to match his linsey shirt and wrinkled pants.

"Rurales, wasn't it?"

"No. Yaquis."

"That's bad."

"They take it out of a man," Rafe Connors said.

"In the worst sort of way."

"They got part of my leg. They got all of my nerve, I reckon."

"I can't believe that. I mind when you was with the Rangers and the Hadley crowd treed a town. You took four of 'em."

"I was chasin' the rest of the crowd down to Mexico when the Injuns got me. Wasn't supposed to cross the Border, as you know. So the Rangers hadda fire me, no pension, nothin'."

"So you come up here."

"And Señor Cuesta give me a job. I tried wranglin'. Couldn't make a go of it." He limped a step looking past Buchanan, shaking his head. "I can ride. Maybe I can still shoot. But it ain't in here." He tapped his chest.

Buchanan said gently, "A man might lose it. But he can find it again."

"The Yaquis make the Apache look like Sunday School

kids. How I got away I'll never know, draggin' my leg. Got picked up by miners." He shuddered. "It was mighty awful, Buchanan."

Patricia Ann said, "I never knew, Rafe. You never told nobody around here."

"You folks been mighty good to me. I ain't about to forget it. But—all I'm good for is . . ."

Suddenly, Rafe lunged forward on his good leg. He slammed into Patricia Ann. She fell against Buchanan, who grabbed for her, staggering back into an empty stall. Rafe flattened himself on the floor of the stable. There was an unmistakable buzz of a bullet. The low sound of a report echoed to the west. Buchanan recovered, slammed the barn doors in one mighty effort. Two more shots followed, striking through the wood but missing the occupants of the stable.

"I can still see sunlight on a rifle barrel," Rafe Connors said. "They don't want you around, Buchanan. They won't rest while you're in the countryside."

"You're bleedin'," Patricia Ann said. "You're hit."

Buchanan went to his saddlebag. He took out several articles, found a small, wrapped package. He took a clean rag and tenderly wiped the bleeding ear of Connors. He applied alcohol as the old man winced. He immediately smoothed a salve on the nicked portion of the ear.

"Indian girl give it to me," he said. "Fine Creek gal. It heals real quick. Won't even need a bandage."

Connors said, "Thankee, Buchanan. It's a little enough to stop more killin'. The Farmingtons got some people that shoot pretty good."

"Not good enough," Buchanan told him. "I'm goin' out the other doors."

"They might have 'em covered."

"Then they better be real good shots," Buchanan said. "Patricia Ann, you stay here."

Connors went dutifully to the rear doors of the barn. Buchanan mounted. Nightshade snorted, recognizing danger, the need for action. The doors swung open. Man and horse leaped as though shot from a cannon. Buchanan rode into the open.

In a trice he knew the girl was behind him. He yelled, "Circle! Don't charge! Circle!"

He knew the lay of the land. Ranches like the C-R were carved out of the brasada, out of the mesquite, the entanglement of a thousand thorns and briars. The brush must be held back and the Cuestas had not been able to do so for several years. The shooters were firing from the safety of heavy cover. He could barely make out the glint of gunbarrels as he fired offhand, riding Indianlike in a series of short parabolas.

The fire was returned. It was an uneven affray, with Buchanan and the girl in the open and the attackers concealed. Yet the girl was obeying and she was shooting. She came into Buchanan's view, leaning on the far side of the horse, firing from beneath its well-trained neck and head.

Still the shooting from the brush continued. Then a window in the house was thrown open. Two rifle barrels shone in the early morn. Consuela and Molly had joined the small war. Buchanan edged closer in his circling ride. He picked a target. He sat the saddle like a rock, pressing the trigger of the Remington.

There was a shout from afar. Then there was the crashing of brush. The girl and the two women in the house continued to lay down a barrage. Buchanan called to them.

"That's enough. They hightailed it."

Patricia Ann rode close and asked, "How do you reckon that they're gone?"

"I know that kind. One gets hurt, they turn tail, 'specially if they had no luck. Lucky the sun was in their eyes somewhat, them coming from the west."

She said sadly, "No use tryin' to track 'em. We ain't dressed for it and they know the brush. They got to be them gunhands that Farmington's been bringin' in."

"Not the Farmingtons themselves?"

She said, "Not riskin' their necks the like of this."

"Maybe you're right."

"Listen, there's a town down the road. Yaqui, it's called. You know it?"

"Not much of a burg."

"They got a lawman name of Wallace. Rusty Wallace."

"Uh-huh. Rusty is another old-timer. He ain't crooked far's I recall."

"No. He's just worn out and he don't like Mexicans and this was the Cuesta layout. He won't help much. On the other hand he won't stand for no outright shenanigans."

"But what he don't know won't hurt him. Right?"

"Yeah," she said. Her mother was coming from the house, rifle in hand, clad in a serape and her nightgown. "Now I'm goin' to catch it."

Molly was already talking. "You, Patricia Ann, what you think you're doin'? You aimin' to be a shootist or somethin'? You get down off that horse and back to the house."

Patricia Ann said mildly, "I aim to show Buchanan where the boys are tryin' to chouse some beef for us."

"Who asked you to do such?"

"Nobody."

Molly glared at Buchanan. "She's too young to take such chances. Wonder you both wasn't killed just now."

"Wasn't for Rafe we might have been before we got out of the stable," Buchanan told her.

"Rafe? Rafe Connors?" There was wonder in her voice.

Buchanan said mildly, "Saved us from the first shots."

"You didn't see him fightin' any, though, did you?"

"Not necessary. He's had his day." Buchanan came down from the saddle. "I would like to get some leggins and gear on me and go out and take a look-see. I think Patricia Ann might go along. There's some figurin' to do. I don't find her such a dumb kid."

Molly softened. She looked aslant at her daughter. "Well, Tom. If you say so. Consuela and me can handle it here. They got a cookie and chuck wagon out there someplace. She can find it for you. But I doubt you'll see anything any good. It's too late to make a herd. I know it. I kept hopin', but what with the Farmingtons makin' trouble and plumb shiftlessness . . ." She spread her hands and turned toward the house. She moved slowly, going through the kitchen door, closing it silently behind her.

"She feels right low," Patricia Ann offered.

"Let's get on some clothes for the brush," Buchanan said. "Let's make a pasear anyway."

"Ma's right. But you got to see it," she agreed.

They went into the bunkhouse. Rafe Connors was before them. He was mending a heavyweight jerkin with a long needle and heavy thread. He said, "Dobey's the biggest in our crew. Maybe I can make this fit you, Buchanan. There's extry leggins and all. You might leave some red if you try to find C-R cows."

Buchanan replied, "I'm wearin' blue today." The reference was to his neckerchief. "Leavin' red" was a term applied to the vaqueros who rode hard through the tangled brush and were snagged by thorns. Buchanan had seen many a shred of cloth, both red and blue in the days when he had aided the Cuestas in rounding up their stock.

The leggins—never called "chaps" in brush country—were not quite large enough, but Buchanan pulled them on to protect his legs. He regretted that he had no tapaderos for his stirrups, but then one couldn't have everything. He found gauntlets that were tight but useable. He looked for an old hat—he had lost a fine Stetson once pursuing a longhorn through a morass when a low-hanging branch had snatched it away.

The girl had her own equipment, he noted, especially fitted to her shapely, muscular form. She was, he thought, an amazing girl, hugely attractive when she was animated, slightly sullen looking when in repose.

And why not, he thought. There was no social life for these two Cuesta ladies, except what they made for themselves on this ranchero in the brasada. There were no men who could possibly attract them—plus the fact that they had to be constantly on guard against the Farmingtons and any stray waddies who might wander this way. There were good people in the land, but the Cuestas were mainly isolated from them and from the town of Yaqui.

He would have to investigate the situation in town, he reminded himself. He would have to poke his nose into more things than he cared to consider at this time. But he was committed, verbally and mentally.

Now the girl was grinning at him. "You are outsize, Buchanan. You look like a stuffed grizzly."

The outer clothing was indeed tight upon his two-hundred-and-forty-pound frame. He said, "I feel like it."

Rafe Connors said hesitantly, "You sure you wanta ride that black into the brush?"

"If I didn't, he'd bite me," Buchanan told him. "Besides, Nightshade's been here before."

They went outdoors and the girl swung aboard Blue with the expert ease of the born rider. She said, "Best let me lead the way. I think I know where there's a couple head of ours."

"Uh-huh." Buchanan forked Nightshade. They rode toward the heavy brush to the east.

Joe Glass, a black rider, was bleeding. Judson Farmington ignored him, glaring at Symes and Brogan, who stood before him like two schoolboys.

"You missed him? You had him in your sights and missed him?"

"He come at us like he's crazy," said Symes, the taller gunslinger. "I swear I had him. I dunno how he got away with it."

"From what I hear he's a target nobody could miss," the old man snarled. "What in hell kind of people have I hired? I thought you were accomplished gunmen."

"We're wanted in Montana and Wyoming," said Brogan, who was bandy-legged and feisty. "It ain't for stealin' ice cream from kids."

Symes added hastily, placating, "Buchanan, that's a name in the West. That's a real bad man."

Farmington snapped, "So his name scared you."

Brogan showed tobacco stained teeth. "Scared ain't it, Mr. Farmington. Buchanan's got his ways. We got ours. And we better patch up Joe. He's got a real reason for gettin' Buchanan now."

"Go and think it over," said Farmington. "Think hard. Because your salaries are too high for inept performance."

They helped Joe Glass to the bunkhouse some distance removed from the porch where the Farmingtons sat in rocking chairs. A servant brought tall glasses of whiskey and soda water, clinking with ice. The two men drank. Hal Farmington held his tongue, waiting as always for his father to take the lead.

After a long wait, Judson Farmington demanded, "Are those two other worthless bums on the job?"

"Wills and Jones are tracking Buchanan," said Hal.

"And will they shoot this monster Buchanan?"

"They do not have orders to do so. You gave the orders to shoot him to those three—who failed."

"And you believe Buchanan might lead us to the treasure?"

"I believe if anyone can it would be Buchanan or someone like him."

The old man drank deeply; then his face altered, he actually smiled, his thin lips spreading cautiously, as though by great effort. "You don't want him killed until you can fight him again, do you?"

"I can handle him if I have the opportunity."

Farmington's attempt at levity slackened. "You really believe you can defeat this phenomenon of the Western frontier? With fists or gun? Or both?"

"I will take my chances." Hal Farmington bit the inside of his mouth until the blood ran. The tone of the old man's voice again was driving him insane.

"That would be your ambition," the voice lashed at him. "Violence. Wipe out your uselessness with a great deed against a legend. Is Buchanan a legend?"

"I don't know," said the young man stiffly. "I only know what the men tell me."

"And the girl? You think the trollop believes it?"

"Patricia Ann may or may not believe it. She has

plenty of chance to find out, since he is staying at the Cuesta ranch."

"You are a fool," said Farmington contemptuously. "You will always be a fool. And the quicker I get you out of this benighted land and back where you belong the better for all of us."

"But you want me to marry Patricia Ann?"

"Marry her, yes. Live your life with her—never!"

"I see. You want me to marry her, then leave her after we secure the treasure."

"Of course, you nitwit! Imagine her in Boston!"

Hal did not reply. He finished his drink and arose. "I'd better look at Joe's wound."

"Yes. You did waste some time in medical study. I do forget. You failed at so many things."

Hal Farmington made a stiff little bow, turned and walked away. His father was calling for the servant to bring him another drink. Hal's head hurt with trying to contain his anger, his frustration.

He had entertained ideas he did not dare express, of course. He had thought of marrying the luscious Patricia Ann and combining the two ranches and discovering the buried treasure and reigning over an empire in Texas while his father returned East. He had been foolish enough to allow himself such a dream.

Truly, he had known better. He had never underestimated the greed of his father. He was aware that the domination of the father over the son was part of a sort of mania that possessed the elder Farmington. Still, he could not prevent himself from dreaming.

He entered the bunkhouse. Glass was groaning under the ministrations of Symes and Brogan. He went close and examined the wound.

It was in the shoulder and the bullet had gone all the

way through. The gunmen had already drawn a clean handkerchief through the hole. Hal Farmington asked for bandages, usually available in the form of old, clean sheets. He applied salve to the area around the bleeding flesh, then dribbled whiskey into the wound. He bandaged skillfully.

Glass grunted and said, "Thank you, Boss."

The other two gunslingers sat on their bunks and watched. Farmington finished the job and stepped back.

Brogan said, "You got a neat way with it, Mr. Hal. Hope you're around when I catch one."

"Tell me about Buchanan."

Glass said, "We got 'em pinned down. Then he come on a big, black hoss. He come like the devil's ridin' with him. He come straight at us. Then the gal come, and the lady, and the Mex gal out the window, every which of a way."

Farmington said, "Right at you, eh?"

"He don't give a damn," Brogan told him. "He gets the wind up he'll charge hell with a bucket o' water."

"I heard tell of him years back," agreed Symes. "I tell you, Mr. Hal, he's one hiyu bastid."

"If we brought him down, the law would be on us, then. A man like that, people would be looking for him, looking for whoever killed him."

"The law's lookin' for us now," said Brogan. "Like I done told your pa. Only your pa's bound to have the man killed. Wisht he'd try it his own self."

"Oh, he probably will," said the son. "He's no coward, believe me."

"I believe you. But he's an old man and he ain't gun quick and waylayin' Buchanan is what we just tried."

Hal Farmington nodded. "Yes. But I don't want him killed."

"You'd go agin your pa?" Brogan laughed shortly. "He'd skin us and hang our hides out to dry—if we let him."

"Alive. Then I could take care of him."

They stared at him. Three pairs of eyes showed utter disbelief. Hal Farmington went into a rage mindful of his father.

"I tell you I can beat him. With my fists or with a gun. I don't believe in this legend. All I need is a chance to prove myself!" He stalked out of the bunkhouse.

The three men exchanged glances. Joe Glass managed a grin.

"Now that's somethin'. I'd sure like to see him and Buchanan go at it."

"I know where my money'd be," said Brogan.

"The boy can fight pretty good," Joe Glass said.

"He's a big piece of bull wind," Brogan said. He chuckled. "You reckon Buchanan would hire us if we quit here and asked him?"

Symes shook his head. "Forget it. Farmington's payin' us good. We do what he says, we're okay."

"The old man's a real turd. The boy's got his brains in his butt. If they didn't have a line on that buried treasure . . ."

"You don't have to like 'em," Symes reminded him. "All you got to do is your job of workin' for 'em."

Joe Glass said, "This here hurts."

"You're lucky," Brogan told him.

"Yeah? Well, whatever y'all think, I'm goin' against Buchanan sooner or later," said Joe Glass. "He won't be the first big man I cut down."

"He could be the last," Symes said gloomily.

"Joe's right," Brogan said. "They don't come too big to stop bullets."

"It hurts," Joe Glass repeated. "I'll be after him soon's as I can handle a gun."

Brogan went to his bunk and brought out another bottle of whiskey. He poured into tin cups, a good four ounces for each of them. They sat and brooded, knowing it would not be long before the Farmingtons had another unpleasant job for them to perform.

Nightshade followed the blue horse through the maze of mesquite with its thorns—retama, with its deceptive yellow flowers; junco, naked and menacing, upon which butcher birds lighted, then flapped away. The girl rode like a Comanche, swaying, ducking under branches, swerving to avoid the stabs of the brasada thickets when possible, tearing into them when necessary. He took his share of the ripping undergrowth but the black horse knew his way by instinct, avoiding serious damage.

Small, lean longhorns ran before them. The balsamlike odor of huajilla from a nearby field came to their nostrils. The half-dozen steers fled, and between them they chivvied the animals to the field.

Buchanan saw them gather, then, with Jimson and Harder tending the fire while three young cowboys worked at the branding. The wild ones from the brush scrambled into the tamed herd and milled about, unsure, unable to escape as the girl helped to round them up. The youngsters roped the most restive, threw him down. The hot iron sizzled as the calf bellowed.

The girl reined in alongside Buchanan and they surveyed the scene. Buchanan shook his head.

"It's a pitiful poor bunch," he said.

"Worse'n that," agreed Patricia Ann.

"Your men ain't top hands."

"They're as bad as the cows." She hunched in the

saddle. "Furthermore, the Farmingtons have got the other big ranchers against us."

Buchanan swung down and went among the little herd, examining a creature here and there. He came back to the girl.

"No sign of hoof and mouth. A tick or two, nothing dangerous. Where's the roundup?"

"On a few miles," she said, pointing to the hills.

"We'll mosey over and take a look-see."

He remounted. The girl spoke to Jimson, who nodded vacantly and then lounged, watching them ride away.

They topped a hill and the roundup was in the early stage. Cattle dotted the landscape for a mile, grazing, milling, fat cattle, ready for the trail.

"Some people have good management," Buchanan observed.

"They can hire good men," the girl replied.

A big man on a chestnut horse rode toward them.

"You know this one?" asked Buchanan.

"Baldwin. Head of the Cattlemen's Association," she said.

Buchanan waited until the man had drawn near. Then he said, "Buchanan's the name. Ramroddin' the C-R."

"Howdy, Miss Patricia Ann," the man said. His voice was heavy but polite. "Buchanan? Heard of you."

"People have."

Baldwin said, "Sorry about the C-R herd."

"Nothin' to be sorry about," Buchanan told him. "Bad management makes for bad times."

"I mean about the disease."

Buchanan said, "That's why I'm here. We're not about to try to drive the C-R cattle. But I got a message for you and the Association."

"And that is?"

Buchanan said flatly, "The Farmingtons are liars. And you haven't given the Cuestas the courtesy of findin' out the truth."

"Now, just a minute. . . ."

"Minute my left hind foot," Buchanan barked. "There's no disease in that herd. It ain't fat, it ain't big, it ain't ready for the trail. I reckon you knew that. But usin' hoof and mouth disease for an excuse, that's plain rotten dishonesty."

Baldwin flushed. He lifted a hand. "The Farmingtons have always kept their word with me, Buchanan."

"Because it's in their interest. You'll learn about them before you're through," Buchanan said harshly. "Next year you'll check with the C-R herd. Believe me, you will. Meantime, think it over."

He motioned to the girl. They rode away, leaving Baldwin to stare after them. Patricia Ann giggled.

"It's not funny," Buchanan said.

"The way his mouth fell open when you told him, that was funny."

"You're going to have to hire a good cattleman before long," he told her.

"That means we got to find the treasure."

"Which will take some doin'. Still, there's always a chance." He wanted to keep her spirits up, to give her a chance to believe in good times to come.

She said, "So many people lookin'. And findin' nothin' at all."

"It's there, somewhere. I want to study on several different things. I'll be goin' to town. Yaqui's still the county seat, right?"

"Right." But she was not truly interested. She could not really believe, he thought. She said, "Are you as sticky and hot as me?"

"It wasn't a picnic, ridin' the brush."

"Okay. I'll race you."

She spurred Blue. It was a fine horse but Buchanan reined in the fleet Nightshade, following, watching. She was as good as any horsewoman he had ever seen—or man, either, for that matter, he thought. The girl needed no more education than she had gained on the ranch. She was equipped for the life. The matter of a working foreman, of the money to pay him was paramount, of course, but she would make a fine ramrodder.

The ever-changing Texas weather brought a fierce sun as they rode. The girl was circling, ignoring the way they had traversed. It was noon and Buchanan's stomach had begun to rumble. Still, he followed, not daring to leave the girl alone. They had gone a couple of miles before he realized that they were being followed.

A clump of oaks, recognizable, came into view. Buchanan watched the roan horse dash through a glade. He went into the trees, then reined Nightshade off the narrow trail and into the trees.

Wills and Jones came cautiously into the field beyond the copse, maintaining their distance. They stopped. Buchanan unlimbered his Remington. He chambered a cartridge and elevated the sight.

He fired two shots. Each whistled past the ears of the two Farmington hands. They stood not upon ceremony, departing back into the far edge of the woods with all dispatch.

Buchanan reloaded the rifle and restored it to the scabbard at his knee. He put Nightshade back on the trail through the oaks.

When he came to the pool below the dam the blue horse was swimming. Patricia Ann was astride him. Her outer garments were strewn on the shore. She was splashing and whooping and thoroughly enjoying herself. The horse seemed to be enjoying it as much as the girl, tossing his head, snorting.

Nightshade lunged toward the inviting pool but Buchanan spoke to him, dismounting, bidding him drink his fill but to stay. He removed the rifle and walked back along the path through the trees. He removed his neckerchief; it had been torn by the brambles. He had left an easy trail to follow, he supposed. The Farmington men had remained out of sight while he was debating with Baldwin. Not until they crossed the field had they dared to show themselves. However, he could take no chances of being ambushed here while he frolicked in the pool with the girl and her swimming horse.

He doffed the canvas jerkin and the gauntlets. He slid out of the leggins, bundled the superfluous garments into his saddle roll. At all times he kept an eye on the surrounding woods.

Patricia Ann shouted, "C'mon in, the water's fine."

He shook his head and motioned to her to return to shore. She laughed and rode in a circle, finally going under the waterfall from above the dam.

He sighed and dipped water into his hat and doused himself. He found a clear spot and drank. He washed his face and neck with the neckerchief. There was no motion in the trees. The sun beat down with fierce delight. He remembered hardtack and jerky in his saddlebag, which he had left behind at the ranch. He was very hungry.

The girl finally pointed the swimming horse to the shore. Her clothing clung to her. Buchanan tried to look her in the eye and failed.

She came ashore and laughed at him. "You never saw a girl before?"

"Plenty of them," he told her dryly. "But seldom soakin' wet."

She tossed her head and pushed back wet hair. "I ain't ashamed of me, Buchanan."

"No reason to be," he said. "But if I don't get back and eat somethin' pretty soon I'll purely fall down."

"I don't believe that," she said. Nevertheless she started for home, wringing herself out as she went. It was a sight to behold, Buchanan admitted to himself.

4

Buchanan rode down the dusty main street of the town of Yaqui on the big black horse. The sun shone on the adobe buildings and they glimmered dully, worn by the elements. There was a saloon labeled McGee's, a general store that also featured hay, grain and feed. The town hall was set apart and a small sign said, *R. Wallace— Marshal.*

There was a bank, a barber shop, a stable and corral, two or three unidentifiable buildings—but no people. A yellow dog scratched itself beneath a wooden awning in front of the marshal's office. Buchanan tied up and dismounted. He was conscious of eyes from within the various edifices. A wagon rolled in from the west.

A sign on the door of the lawman's retreat spelled out *Back later,* in irregular print. Buchanan walked fifty yards to the saloon.

It was cool and dark inside and he squinted, making

his way to the bar. A tall man with a drooping mustache regarded him, unsmiling. There were a dozen men in the place, seated at tables.

Buchanan said, "Have you got cold beer?"

"I got it," said the mustachioed man.

Buchanan put a silver dollar on the bar, which was scarred by long misuse. "I'll have one."

Behind him a voice said, "Buchanan?"

He turned, hooking his elbows, peering. "That you, Rusty? Can't see too good in here."

An aging man got up from a table and came to the bar. He was clean-shaven; he smelled of the barber shop. He had lined, strangely pale cheeks, a long chin, eyes set deep, thick brows. He wore a star on an open vest.

"It's me. What you doin' here besides causin' a rumpus?"

"Rumpus?"

"Shootin' people and such." Wallace's voice was slow and even and without rancor.

"News does travel fast in this country." The beer was not cold, merely cool. Ice had not come to Yaqui from the northland.

Wallace said, "Not that it's any different from wherever I seen you. For a peaceable man you do get into trouble a heap."

"Someone swear out a warrant?" asked Buchanan.

"Not yet." The man behind the bar was pouring from a whiskey bottle. Wallace accepted the drink, balanced himself alongside Buchanan. "Seems like you and the Farmingtons are at it."

"Leave us say they have been at me."

"I heard. So far, it ain't any of my business. Truth to tell, I hope it never will be. Got somethin' on your mind?"

No one in the bar had spoken except the marshal and Buchanan. Through the door Buchanan could see that now there were people in the street. There were Mexican women and men, a private citizen or two, children and more dogs. There were always dogs in these towns. The wagon had stopped opposite the saloon, the two men on the seat watching and waiting. There had certainly been gossip, word sent ahead by someone, not necessarily the Farmingtons, he thought.

He said, "Uh-huh. Want to walk down to your office?"

The men in the bar were listening with all their ears. Wallace did not glance at them. The barkeeper did not move from his position, leaning arms akimbo.

The marshal said, "Why not?"

They left the saloon. The few people in the street made a path for them. Still, no one spoke. The silence in a town like Yaqui was eerie. Buchanan, as usual, had not worn his gunbelt into the place. He felt naked, walking to the office of the marshal. He went over in his mind what he knew about Wallace.

Back in the trail days Rusty Wallace had been a lawman for various boomtowns. He had been in Dodge with Earp and Masterson, in Abilene with Hickock. He had been a quiet man always, never a domineering officer. He was reputed to have killed several outlaws but had never been in a brawl outside the law that Buchanan knew about.

He was not a gambler. When the trails had slowed down he had vanished from the scene and it was said he had returned to the East from which he had emigrated after the Civil War. No one knew anything more about him.

The office was large enough, plainly furnished, a few yellowing wanted posters on the wall, a gunrack meticulously kept, a door leading to a cell or two at the rear. Another door led into the courthouse and against it was a cracked leather chair. Wallace went behind a desk, sat down, opened a drawer, and took out a bottle. He was pouring into shot glasses when he suddenly stopped and began to cough.

There was blood on his handkerchief when the paroxysm was ended. He did not try to conceal it. He looked broodingly at Buchanan, wadded the kerchief, and put it in a large wooden box already tainted with bloodstains.

"Consumption," he said with effort. "Oughta be on the high place in New Mexico. Your place."

Buchanan asked, "How bad is it?"

"Gettin' worse. You know, it's easy gettin' old. But bein' old, that's rotten."

"You had a pretty good life." Buchanan scarcely knew what to say. His own health was so enormously good that he had no experience on which to draw.

"Good enough." Wallace wiped his lips with the back of his hand. "But I'll tell you somethin' nobody knows. I got a daughter."

"Whereabouts?"

"Back home. Near Boston."

"Boston?" He immediately thought of the Farmingtons. "That's a far piece."

"Ain't seen her since—oh, ten years ago. She's married to a farmer, got two of her own kids. They're good, honest people. But they ain't makin' it too good. Hard rock farm in Massachusetts. Sam ain't got the gumption to move. His father left him the place, he figures it's good enough for him and his."

"Uh-huh." There was something behind this revelation. Buchanan waited.

"You wonder why everybody's so quiet like here in Yaqui?"

"I got a notion. It's somethin' to do with the Cuesta treasure."

"Cuesta's treasure? Anybody finds it ain't goin' to ask whose it may have been. Every man child is out for it, one way or another. Special since the Farmingtons come here and began lookin' at maps and all."

Buchanan said slowly, "Now, that's just what I aim to do, Rusty. Look at some courthouse maps."

"Figured on that." Wallace made a gesture. "They pay me eighty a month here. Can't send much back to the daughter on that. I don't know how much more time I got and them grandchildren and all. The Farmingtons, they made me offers. All kinds. Got two messages just afore you come in."

"Arrest me? Or kill me?"

"One said jail. The other said kill."

Buchanan grinned. "Makin' it hard on you, ain't they?"

"If they offered cash," Wallace said. "I dunno."

"But they offered you a share."

"When they find the treasure."

Buchanan tilted his head. "You want me to make an offer, is that it?"

"I know you, Buchanan. You get what you go after if you want it bad enough."

Buchanan considered. Then he said, "Tell you what. If I find it, the Cuestas get it. If you stay out of it I can guarantee you somethin'."

"How much?"

"How would I know?"

"I got to have enough for the kids."

"No way I can say how much."

Wallace coughed, controlled the spasm. He clutched at his middle with his right hand.

Buchanan put the toe of his boot against the edge of the desk. He pushed hard. Wallace's chair rolled back and hit the wall. Buchanan went over it like a big cat and reached down.

The marshal's grasp on the revolver was lax. Buchanan straightened up with it in his hand. He gently pulled away the desk. Wallace collapsed atop it, again coughing.

Buchanan sat back down. He weighed the gun. It was an old Frontier-model Colt. He emptied it of bullets and slid it across the top of the desk.

When Wallace had recovered, Buchanan asked, "Well which was it to be?"

"Jail," murmured the marshal. "I couldn't . . . couldn't . . . "

Buchanan said, "Uh-huh. I believe you. Now listen to me—stay clean and I'll see you get somethin' if and when. It'll be a help, whatever it is. But Rusty—stay clean. I don't ask for help. I just ask a square deal."

Wallace nodded. He sat huddled in the chair, an old man clinging to a tiny hope for others, not himself.

Buchanan said, "Now I'll take a look at those maps."

Wallace gestured toward the door. Buchanan removed the chair, heard hinges creak as he went into a small entryway, then into the high-ceilinged room that served as a courtroom. There were benches and beyond them another door. He went into the next room, which was tiered with wooden cabinets lined with drawers. A middle-aged woman stared at him, uneasy. She was well enough dressed, plain-featured, buxom.

"Name's Buchanan," he said. "Like to look at some old records and maps."

"I am Mrs. Bascomb." She was still nervous. "I work here, for the county."

"Yes'm." She was fumbling with a sheaf of papers. He smiled at her. "Reckon you got the Cuesta maps and all right there, huh?"

She said, "There was a request for them."

"I expect everybody in town has had a look at 'em. I'll just borrow them for a while."

"You can't take them out of here," she said defensively. "It's against the law."

"Not aimin' to do any such of a thing." He still smiled, reaching for the file.

She relaxed. Few women could resist the Buchanan grin. She handed over the thick packet. Buchanan retreated into the judicial chamber, climbed up on the judicial bench and spread out the papers on the surface of the judicial rostrum. Mrs. Bascomb came timidly to watch from below, seating herself in the first row of benches.

He looked down at her. "You friendly to Rusty Wallace?"

She flushed. "He boards with me. The marshal isn't a well man."

"You talk like maybe you were a schoolteacher."

"I'm what they have. I taught Patricia Ann—what little she'd bother to learn."

"Uh-huh." It was hard to imagine the ranch girl in a schoolroom. "You know Molly, then?"

"I'm a friend of hers."

"Good." He returned his attention to the papers. They meant nothing for the most part—a recording of a deed; some business matters; outline of the Cuesta holdings. He found what he was looking for, a map of the ranch in detail, including the surrounding terrain, the stream which led to the dam, the place where Benito Cuesta had been ambushed.

Actually, he believed the maps to be useless. Not only did riverbeds change their course, but in the brasada a jungle could have grown over the hiding place of the Cuesta treasure in far less than a hundred years. His only hope of the least of clues lay in the last line of the message on the old parchment, "Look for water. . . ." If he could learn where the stream had changed, there might possibly be traces of a dried bed beneath. The heavy gold and jewelry might have sunk and been only covered with a few tons of earth and undergrowth.

"Are these the oldest maps you got?" he asked.

"People have been going over them for many years," said the woman. He thought she was being evasive. Something to do with Wallace, he guessed.

He made mental notes—his frontiersman's mind needed no more. He stacked the papers in a neat heap. He came down to the floor and handed them to Mrs. Bascomb.

He asked, "Was it the Farmingtons who wanted them today?"

"Why . . . yes."

He laughed. "They sure are scared I'll find something. You better look out. They might have a mind to steal 'em."

"I'll tell Rusty . . . the marshal," she said.

"You do that. Have a nice day." He smiled at her again and went to the street door of the courthouse.

He walked straight into a circle of people who were obviously waiting for his appearance. They had him cut off on three sides with the building behind him. There was a carriage pulled by a team of matched grays directly before him.

He looked at an old man and recognized him at once

for Judson Farmington. The description fitted, an aging goat, trimmed beard and all. Hal Farmington was climbing down on the other side of the equipage. There was a small, sustained murmur from the crowd, the sound of expectation.

Behind him he heard the quick tap of Mrs. Bascomb's heels as she went to the door leading into Wallace's office. He did not turn his attention from the Farmingtons.

The old man spoke in a harsh, high voice. "So you are the great Buchanan?"

"That's my name." He watched Hal Farmington come around behind the wagon, stretching his ribbed buckskin gloves tight on big hands. "Better keep an eye on your son, there. He might get himself hurt."

"Or, perhaps, it may be you who gets hurt?" There was calculation in the eyes of the old man. There was certainly no fear.

Buchanan said, "You hold yourself mighty high, don't you, Mr. Farmington?" He was watching the slow approach of Hal Farmington, a cautious but meaningful advance. In his turbulent life he had encountered dozens and dozens of dangerous people, so that he recognized the breed. Farmington senior was rattlesnake bad. The son was the lesser threat but like all weak men there was in him a very real danger. They could be a deadly pair, each in his own way.

There was a question in his busy mind: How to deal with the situation under the eyes of the entire town of Yaqui? He would have to think fast. Hal was wearing his gun beneath his arm. Even as he flicked a glance to make certain, the old man seized a sawed-off shotgun and held it across his knees.

"I *am* mighty high, Buchanan," Judson Farmington

said. "And this time I aim to see fair play. No kicking, you understand?" He stared at the crowd. "And no interference from anyone. Man to man is the way it must be."

"Man to boy," said Buchanan sadly.

"Go after him, son," commanded Farmington, his hand on the trigger of the greener.

No crowd would interfere in a fistfight, Buchanan knew. Rather, the people would savor the showdown. Everyone loved a good encounter between two men intent on fisticuffs. There was no sign of the marshal appearing to restore order. There was a slight crowding in of the spectators, eager for the show. Hal put up his hands in approved fashion, elbows bent, gloved fists high. The ribs of the buckskin would cut if he landed on bare skin. He was, Buchanan thought, a headhunter, Eastern-style.

His mind made up, he gathered himself. Hal Farmington came in with a shrewd feint of the right, then a left jab aimed at the face. Buchanan had met this maneuver a thousand times training with Coco Bean, the great Negro fighter.

He blocked the jab, warding it off, then moved to his left, away from the menacing right hand. He ducked inside under Hal's guard. He picked up the younger man and flung him.

Hal sailed through the air. He landed, as Buchanan had intended, practically in the lap of his father. Buchanan followed. Yelling to the crowd, "Stand back, there!" he slapped at the withers of the gray horse nearest him. He yelled, "Whooooeee! Go, you plugs, go!"

He stepped back. People were scurrying frantically for safety. The team was bolting. The shotgun flew from the hands of Farmington. Buchanan caught it before it could fall to earth and explode.

Judson Farmington rocked on the seat as the team bolted. The crowd was staring, startled, nonplussed. But Buchanan came around with the gun leveled.

Hal Farmington had bounced free of the carriage. He was on his feet, off balance, reaching under his arm for his gun.

Buchanan said softly, "This here thing would blow you half in two, young fella."

Hal raised his hands above his head. Buchanan cradled the shotgun and approached him, keeping his gaze steadily upon Farmington's eyes. He plucked the gun from its underarm holster with the speed of a magician. He stepped back.

The young man said, "Put the guns down. I'll fight you."

A hoarse voice from the crowd said, "That's fair, Buchanan. Ain't you goin' to fight him?"

It was a thought to consider. Buchanan said, "You got sand, young fella, I'll say that for you."

"I can whip you any time, any day!" Farmington was pale but he did not seem afraid.

The hoarse voice said again, "Mebbe Buchanan's scared."

He located the man who was speaking. It was McGee from the saloon. Several of the men were now joining in, agreeing with the barkeeper. Some of the women scuttled away, others remained.

Buchanan said, "Nothin' was ever decided by one man beatin' on another—exceptin' it was for a purse."

"I'll put up a hundred," insisted McGee.

"I don't fight for money. I'm a peaceable man," Buchanan told him.

Farmington said heatedly, "No money. Just you and me, Buchanan. Right now."

Buchanan made his decision. He shook his head preparatory to speaking. Marshal Wallace came out of his office holding a kerchief to his mouth. Mrs. Bascomb was behind him.

Wallace said, "There'll be no fightin' on the streets of this town. I've said it before and I say it again."

"It's a showdown," McGee said. "They got a right to see who's best."

"You get back where you belong," Wallace told him.

There was a resentful murmur throughout the crowd. The marshal stood his ground, his guns hanging low on his thin flanks. Buchanan handed the shotgun to him, flipped the cylinder, emptied Hal Farmington's gun, and returned it.

McGee retreated. He called, "I still say Buchanan ain't showin' the sand he talks about."

The crowd slowly dispersed, returning to the silence that Buchanan had noted upon his arrival. Farmington shifted from one foot to the other. There was the sound of carriage wheels and Judson Farmington drove the gray team back down the main street. Dust eddied from beneath the wheels and people scattered. The old man's cheeks showed spots of color. He spoke in his harsh manner to his son.

"So. You haven't destroyed the legend. The same old story, isn't it? Get up here."

For an instant young Farmington hesitated. Then he went, pale and shaken, to the carriage and climbed up beside his father.

Farmington stared at Buchanan. "I'll be interested in you from now on. Watch your step."

Buchanan said, "You know so much—why don't you go home and count steps yourself?"

A lingering woman tittered. Two of her friends joined

in. Farmington seemed about to explode. Then he slapped the reins and the team leaped against the traces. The Farmingtons rode out of town.

Buchanan said, "He forgot his shotgun."

"He'll send for it," Wallace replied. "He's great on sendin' for things."

They walked to the hitching post where Nightshade waited. Wallace was smiling. Mrs. Bascomb went into the courthouse.

The marshal said, "The town still listens. McGee, I believe now he sold out to the Farmingtons. His men do their boozin' with him."

Buchanan said, "Hold her steady, Rusty. And watch your back."

"I been doin' that for many a year." The marshal frowned. "If only those kids back East could inherit somethin' from me I'd be okay."

"Keep hopin'. And keep tryin'. And thanks for breakin' up the ruckus. It wasn't the right time to go at young Farmington."

"It might've been a better time than if the old man had a real holt on you."

"I'm thinkin' on that," said Buchanan. He reached into a saddlebag and took out his gunbelt and fastened it around his waist. "I'll be seein' you. Maybe soon."

He mounted and rode out of Yaqui. It was still silent along the main street.

He rode slowly, his mind turning over what had transpired, what he had learned. Rusty Wallace was an uncertain vessel, he thought, but a man who had always lived by high standards. He was driven now by the needs of others, and this could very well cause changes in his thinking and actions.

McGee was obviously a danger and, as the owner of the

only saloon, a factor to be considered. Probably Wallace would keep an eye on him—they were diametrically opposed as human beings. And there was Mrs. Bascomb, a possible influence as schoolteacher and custodian at the courthouse.

Then there were the Farmingtons. The old man was an Easterner who had come to rape the western country, Buchanan thought. He would never be a part of the land, he was a depredator. He had brains and enough money to hire desperados. He was not a coward. He was dangerous down to his shiny Boston boots.

The son was different. Cowed by his father, he also did not lack courage, as had been demonstrated. He believed he could whip Buchanan in a fair fight. He was willing to try. Yet he was tricky and callous, as witness the scene at the dam when Buchanan had first encountered him. He might have a streak of cruelty, inherited from his father.

Neither was to be trusted as far as Buchanan could throw a bull by the tail.

Buchanan wrenched himself back to his present situation. He was riding a road behind the Farmingtons. It was possible that Judson carried a rifle as well as a shotgun. It was not impossible that Hal would be forced by his father into trying a showdown with the underarm .38. They were capable, perhaps, of an ambush.

This brought another train of thought. The maps at the courthouse had proven nothing—but there was a couple of phases of the last expedition of Benito Cuesta that could bear investigation.

Remembering the terrain from his last visit to the brasada country, he turned Nightshade off the road. There was a precarious path through the underbrush that led to a trail. If he could get to it, the trail would lead him past

the dam where he had first seen Patricia Ann and up into
the flat land where the massacre of her father had oc-
curred. He rode cautiously, watchful for sign of other
humans.

Judson Farmington pulled the lathered team off the
road. He had been driving at a furious pace all the way
from Yaqui. Without speaking Hal jumped down, plucked
handfuls of dried furze, and began wiping down the pant-
ing horses.

Judson's voice came out in a ferocious, animallike
growl. "They laughed at me."

Hal continued his task.

"Those peasants, those greasers, they laughed."

Still no remark from the son. Judson reached behind
him and picked up a finely tooled Remington sporting
rifle. He levered a cartridge into the chamber. Hal paused,
staring.

"You're not thinking of ambushing Buchanan?"

"I will know what to do when he rides up to us."

"Buchanan won't give you a chance. If he sees us here
beside the road he'll turn off. And then he might come in
at us from another direction. He's a plainsman. They tell
me he knows all the Indian tricks."

"Buchanan will ride to us," Judson said. "He will con-
front us. He will not avoid a challenge."

"How can you be sure of that?"

"I looked into his eyes. I saw him for what he is. A
romanticist. A man who lives by a code."

"You think his code invites him to suicide?"

"I think he will be ready. He will know that I won't
shoot him down like the overgrown dog that he is."

Hal went back to the job of cooling off the horses. He

knew better than to debate with his father once Judson had made up his mind.

Judson went on, "He made a fool of me. And a double fool of you, handling you as if you were a child."

"You haven't felt the strength of the man," muttered Hal. "In a fair fight I can whip him. But if it came to wrestling I have no chance."

"Then I would advise you to use that fast gun of which you are so proud."

Hal said, "Either way, I shall certainly try him."

"Try him! Try! You pusillanimous idiot, you must do more than try!"

"I can beat him," Hal stated. "I know I can. I have more brains, better training. No uncouth frontier person is better than I am."

"You had better do so." There was deep passion in his father's voice. "One of us must. I have a deep personal interest in bringing down this man. You understand?"

"I understand, Father."

"He has interfered with our plans. He has made me a subject of ridicule to the oafs of that miserable town. He is a present and future danger to us."

"Yes, sir."

"This time you must not fail. When he comes this way I shall force him to fight you. If you fail me, I shall arrange his demise."

"That would be murder, Father."

"Not the way I shall manage it. It will be an accident." Farmington paused, then said thoughtfully. "In fact I shall put my mind to that question."

"What question, father?"

"A manner in which Buchanan can be made either to appear to destroy himself—or be destroyed by fate."

Hal said meekly, "It will take some thought. But I am sure you can manage it."

"You have more confidence in me than I have in you. Which is unfortunate. Still, I will prevail."

Judson nursed the rifle, brooding, his sallow face lined with thought and rage, twisted with emotions from the deep well of his hatred.

5

Buchanan rode a short distance from the road and found a tree he could climb. It was not a very tall tree and it was prickly like all the vegetation in that land, but he managed. When he had reached as high as he could go he looked back down at the road. He saw the Farmington buggy pulled to one side, the two men settled into a waiting position.

He descended the tree, climbed aboard Nightshade, and went along the narrow trail. He did not feel that he was being followed. He rode to the stream and found the copse of oaks. Now he climbed again, taking along his field glasses. He could discern no movement behind him nor in any other point of the compass.

He rode again. He had almost reached the dam when he heard the telltale sound of splashing water. He reined in and there were the girl and Blue, enjoying themselves. The girl appeared to be naked, but he noted that aboard the roan there was a bulky package in a rainproof cover. He sighed and dismounted, allowing Nightshade to drink.

He dipped water, swallowed. The girl was turning over and over in the water, slowly and most gracefully. He had seen porpoises behave in such fashion years back in the Gulf of Mexico. She was as much, or more, at home than she would be on dry land.

She popped beneath the horse, came up on the other side, facing Buchanan. He said, "I thought your mother and me both warned you about bein' out here alone."

Without exposing her body she reached out one long arm. From the peculiar-looking package she drew the second sawed-off shotgun Buchanan had seen that day. Balancing herself on the horn of the saddle she flipped it around, aiming at the brush. The explosion ripped the moist air.

Buchanan said, "Those things are neither accurate nor have they got any range."

She said meekly, "I didn't want to take Ma's rifle."

She started for shore, the shotgun back in place, the horse dutifully following. When she came to the edge, he saw that she was wearing two bandannas about her bosom. When she came ashore she was in the shortest, tightest pair of cutoff Levi's he had ever beheld.

"You like my bathing suit?" she demanded, adjusting the bandannas, which were inadequate.

"It sure is original," he told her.

"It's comfortable. And let me tell you, nobody can keep me away from this place. My pa taught me to swim here. It's the only fun I got. Don't you ever have fun, Buchanan?"

"Uh-huh," he said.

"Can you swim?"

"Every drover has to be able to swim, else he couldn't go across the rivers on the trail."

"You any good at it?"

"Never had to prove much, one way or t'other."

"I'll race you across the dam."

"I just happened to forget my bathing suit," he said. "Besides, I got a few things on my mind."

She sat down on the grass, wringing out her long hair. "What happened in Yaqui?"

He squatted on his heels and told her in detail, told her how the Farmingtons were waiting to bushwhack him. She nodded and when he was finished, she said, "Miz Bascomb, she's all right, I guess. Rusty Wallace ain't much, but he's been honest."

"He's sick."

"I know. Consumption. This ain't good country for him. Why don't he move on to the high places?"

Buchanan said, "A man can't always do what he wants, no matter what ladies think. Now, what I want to do, I want to look over the exact place where your pa was . . . ambushed."

She sobered. "Yes. I been there plenty times. It's not too far, actually. You want to go now?"

"Right now before dark overtakes us."

She said, "Okay. Right now." She took full-length Levi's and a shirt from the package aboard Blue. They were dry, he saw.

"Who figured out that gun-holdin' contraption?" he asked.

"Rafe and me," she said. "Rafe sure knows his knots and things like o' that."

"Rafe knows a heap of things," Buchanan told her.

"He's old and scared."

Buchanan smiled. "He's about my age, Patricia Ann."

"Can't be!"

"He's been through hell and he hasn't been able to come back."

She stared at him wide-eyed. "You're a young man."

Not displeased, he answered, "It's been said. But believe me, it's not true."

She flushed. She said, "I'm dry enough." She arose and quickly slid into the Levi's, socks and boots. Then she turned away and put her arms through the shirt sleeves, managing to remove the damp bandannas. When she turned she was properly attired, but still the tight garments were revealing. "I don't care. You're young enough for me!"

She went quickly to her saddlebag, the newly contrived waterproof sack.

Buchanan said dryly, "I'd slip another shell into that greener if I were you. And mind it's wiped real dry."

"I know enough to do that," she flared. Then, as she did as he suggested, she smiled again. "You are somethin' else, Buchanan. You think of every little old thing, don't you?"

"It keeps a person alive," he told her. He went to Nightshade, picked up the trailing reins. "You ready?"

Now she grinned wickedly, "I'm more'n ready. It's you ain't ready."

Then she was on Blue, going northward past the dam. He was taken aback. She was just a child, he told himself. But his eyes told him something quite different.

The trail led upward, never far from the stream. The topography changed as always in the never dull country of Texas. The brasada lay behind them now; there were oaks and buffalo grass fields where a few longhorns grazed morosely, some of them C-R branded. They climbed steadily until the far hills seemed closer to them than they actually were. The force of the stream increased and there were shallow rapids.

Buchanan wondered what had been in the mind of Benito Cuesta to cause him to make this journey with a small force of retainers. The word "water" on the parchment had, he felt, something to do with it. Yet he could not shake the conviction that the old caravan, under attack, could have dumped the treasure into a fast-running rivulet.

Perhaps Benito had discovered another clue. Perhaps he had been right. It all was a mystery which lacked a key clue.

There was a sudden declivity, no more than a swale. The hills were low but there was heavy brush along the rims. The girl rode into the place and then Blue stopped, as if accustomed to this spot. Patricia Ann turned and looked at Buchanan. There were tears in her eyes.

"This is where Pa died."

He nodded without words. He put Nightshade up the slope of the highest hill, leaving the girl to control her emotions, understanding her grief. When he had reached the hilltop he took out his field glasses and scanned the horizon, taking his time, using great care. Seeing no sign of skulkers he thought that the Farmingtons, waiting on the side of the road, had not yet given orders. A man like Judson would keep a strict line of command. It could be advantageous—or it could lead to gaps in his plans.

Buchanan rode back down the hill. Turning Nightshade loose, he began to examine the ground where the massacre had taken place. Too much time had gone, he thought; there were no signs, nature had taken over. There was the sparse furze, growing thick, a few bare spots, shale and sand.

The girl had wandered off to the edge of the stream a hundred yards away. He preferred to leave her alone with her emotions for that time.

He whistled to Nightshade, who came close. He dug in his saddlebags and found an old, short-handled miner's pick, a relic of days gone by and Mousetrap Mulligan's last adventure. He dug in desultory fashion, unearthing the brush, pulling out the roots, searching the sandy soil.

Patricia Ann returned and watched him. "What do you expect to find? We been over this, the men and Rafe, even, and Ma and me."

"True to tell," Buchanan answered, "I scarcely expect to find anything. Just lookin'."

"Pa was found right over yonder." She pointed and now she was dry-eyed and matter of fact, with a hint of rage in her voice. "He'd been shot twice, once in the head. We think they wounded him, then made sure with the head shot. There was a dead man nearby, someone we didn't know. One of them."

Buchanan went to the spot she indicated. Oddly, it was bare of foliage. He began working around the edges very gently, sifting the loosened soil through his fingers. He heard the girl gasp and looked up at her.

"I know. Hallowed ground."

"It's all right."

He said, "I'm doin' this for the Cuestas. You, your ma and Benito."

"I know," she repeated.

After a moment she knelt down and began to help. She had fine, strong hands, the pink nails half-mooned in white, strangely beautiful for the outdoor girl that he knew her to be. Good blood, he thought, and felt strongly that she and her mother deserved far better than the world afforded them at this time.

She was serious, intent. She hunkered down like a cowboy, her hands busy with the dirt loosened by the pick. One of the buttons on her shirt had come undone and Buchanan averted his gaze. She was not, he conceded, a child.

She said, "Hey. What's this?"

It was round and hard and heavy. Buchanan looked at it, turned it over. He asked quietly, "Do you remember the wound in your father's body?"

"Could I forget it?"

"Was it in the shoulder?"

"That's why we thought he was alive until they pistoled him," she answered.

"Then this bullet could have gone through him."

She nodded, biting her lip. Buchanan put the piece of lead in his pocket. Without the cartridge it could not be useful as evidence, he knew. But it was a shot from a small bore rifle, possibly from a sporting rifle. Judson Farmington would own such a weapon, probably would prefer it to the heavier frontier guns. Nothing could be proven, but Buchanan had begun to construct a court of law in his head, his own law, the law of the frontier.

His pick turned up from time to time a small, round stone. He examined one. The attrition of water over the years could account for this sort of wear, he thought. His mind traveled to his original idea of a stream of water which had altered its course. Perhaps there had been a river down this swale.

He arose and went northward, walking, looking for a possible source. He could not come to a decision. Almost anywhere in the hill country of the West there had been running water at some time in history, he believed.

He went back to the place where Benito Cuesta had been killed. Patricia Ann had fashioned a cairn of the round stones. He helped her replace the dirt; there had been no reason to dig deep in view of the more or less recent time of the event. When they had finished, the spot resembled a grave.

Patricia Ann said, "He's buried in the family cemetery. But this . . . this here is nice."

"Amen," said Buchanan.

"The bullet—it don't mean anything, does it?"

"Not anything you could put a handle on."

She said, "I think we better go home now."

They rode back down the trail. They were each deep in thought; they had nothing to say to each other. The sun was westering and Buchanan was once more aware of hunger. The girl was directly ahead of him. If there was any hint of danger, his sixth sense would warn him, he knew. It seemed a long way back to the C-R Ranch.

They came into the clearing. They reined in, taken utterly by surprise. Molly Cuesta, Consuela and Rafe Connors were lined up against the rear of the house. The carriage of Judson Farmington was backed into the barn door. The old man and his son sat at their ease, rifle and revolver in their respective grasps.

Judson Farmington called, "We've been patiently waiting for you. Don't make a move for a gun, Buchanan. This time you are going to fight for your life."

There was no chance of denying the man. Patricia Ann was in the line of fire. Farmington was demented, Buchanan was certain, at least on one subject, probably two or three more.

"If you'll dismount," said Judson. "My son will accommodate you."

Buchanan got down from Nightshade. He took the chance that the Farmingtons were not fully aware of Western custom by slipping the reins around the horn of the saddle. Only Nightshade knew what that meant—but any horseman knew that a good horse stood with the reins trailing.

Hal Farmington put the revolver on the seat of the carriage, within his father's reach. He leaped to earth. He actually looked triumphant, as though he had finally reached a cherished goal.

Buchanan glanced around. Three men, Glass, Symes, and Brogan, were strategically placed on the perimeter of the backyard. One of them, a black man, had his arm in a sling. The Farmingtons had not waited too long by the road. They had gone home for reinforcements before moving in on the C-R Ranch and its occupants.

"You, girl, down off that horse," said Judson.

Patricia Ann said weakly, "Please . . . I'm scared. . . . Please."

She slid from the saddle, staying close to Blue, cowering. Buchanan reassured her with a word, saw her drop an eyelid. He stepped into the clear.

He said, "Women and unarmed men seem to be your specialty, Farmington. Tell me, what are the rules you mean to set down for this affair?"

"I will dictate the rules. Brogan!"

"Yeah, Boss?"

"You will act as second to my son."

"Okay, Boss." Brogan came forward, holstering his gun. He grinned at Buchanan, a feisty little man, and took his place behind Hal Farmington.

Judson said, "The crippled fellow may act as your second, Buchanan."

Rafe shuffled forward, the picture of mingled fear and hatred. Buchanan motioned him back. Symes and the black man now had them covered, along with the rifle in the hands of Judson. It made the situation seem impossible to alter in any fashion.

Judson said sharply, "You will remove your gunbelt, Buchanan. One false move and you are a dead man."

"And you'll hang," Buchanan told him.

"I will take my chances on that." The old man showed his teeth. "An accident, perhaps. A fire? That old house would burn well, I think."

"You try burnin' an adobe house," Buchanan said and laughed.

Young Farmington stared at the sound of Buchanan's mirth, free and clear. Buchanan handed his gunbelt over and Brogan carried it to Judson, who continued his oration.

"The rules will be collegiate boxing. Not Marquis of Queensbury. There will be no wrestling, none of your mucker tricks, Buchanan. It will be fair and square, a test of skill and strength. I will act as referee from where I sit. You will obey my commands." He gestured with the rifle.

It was a light Remington model, Buchanan noted, as he had expected, a sporting rifle.

He looked around once more, fixing everyone in his or her place. He stepped back to be closer to Rafe Connors.

The lame man whispered, "I got a gun on me. They didn't bother to search me."

Buchanan did not reply. The question remained, would Rafe have the courage to use his weapon in a showdown? Was there something left in the man who had been so severely tortured by the Yaquis?

Judson was going on. "Remove your shirt, Buchanan. I know you Western bullies carry concealed knives."

Buchanan shucked his loose vest and pulled the shirt up over his head. Everyone stared. His muscles rippled, his stomach was flat and ribbed. And there were scars, wounds from engagements up and down the frontier, souvenirs of his many years of doing battle. He saw young Farmington's eyes flicker for an instant.

He hitched at his belt with its wide, ornate belt buckle. What they did not know was that he always carried a derringer concealed beneath the bull's head with its ruby red eyes. He chuckled to himself despite the seriousness of the occasion. The old man thought he knew so much and truly he knew so little.

Still, there were the cohorts. He did not deceive himself about them. They were guns for hire; they knew their business. And he had wounded the black man.

Judson still talked. "Brogan, scratch a fifteen feet square ring."

The gunslinger looked around, saw a rake leaning against the barn wall. He picked it up, set it askew and jumped upon it, breaking the handle. He used a sharp end to pace off and scratch the dirt.

Molly Cuesta burst forth, "You'll pay for that rake, Farmington."

"Gladly." The old man sneered, throwing a coin at her feet. "Now, Buchanan, since you have been known to consort with a nigger prizefighter I am aware that you know the primary rules. No biting or gouging or hitting below the belt."

Buchanan said, "Well, I never did go to college. Didn't learn all those dirty tricks."

"Watch your mouth!" Judson flushed, remembering the laughter in the town of Yaqui. "You will stop fighting any moment that I call time. You will begin on the same signal from me."

"You do think you amount to much," Buchanan said, deliberately goading the man.

"Enough of your insolence," roared Farmington. "Hal, destroy this bully! TIME!"

Hal came dancing. He was light on his feet for a man his size. He held up his hands, leading with the left, circling as Buchanan blocked the punch.

Buchanan moved easily, watching the other man, trying to keep the Farmington people within his range of vision. He had been gifted with great peripheral vision, which had saved his life on more than one occasion. He blocked another left. The muscles in his back glistened as sweat accumulated under the strong beating of the sun.

He made a fast move left, then reversed the position, going right. Hal Farmington moved in. Buchanan struck with his left fist. He landed high on the cheekbone.

Hal staggered, then went down. Blood flowed from his face where Buchanan's hard knuckles had caught him.

"Time!" bellowed Judson. His grip on the rifle tightened and for a moment Buchanan feared he would fire. Then he regained control as Brogan made a knee upon which young Farmington sat dazedly.

Buchanan stood in his corner next to Rafe Connors. He whispered, not moving his lips, "If I knock him out the old man may lose his grip."

"If you don't—you may kill him."

Buchanan slid his gaze around the yard. Molly was crouched against the wall in the shade. Consuela wrung her hands in her apron. Patricia Ann rested her right hand on the package aboard the roan. The gunmen were alert, expressionless, save for the black man. His eyes were fixed on Buchanan and they plainly showed hatred.

Judson Farmington was leaning forward, speaking to his son. "Get up and show that you can whip him!"

Still, he did not call time. He was giving his son plenty

of chance to recuperate. Buchanan took a deep breath and turned it all over in his busy mind. He was afraid that Patricia Ann would make an unwise move. He was uncertain of Rafe. Either the black man or Judson would cut loose if there was a spark to set them off.

He decided it was best to play for time. Judson now roared his command to action. Hal came out more carefully, dancing on his toes, feinting, then ducking when Buchanan struck with a straight left. They moved like two wary animals for several moments. Brogan yelled, "Get at it, Boss. Get him!"

Hal came in with a long left. Buchanan allowed it to slide over his shoulder, countering inside. His fist hit the ribs and Hal went backward. All the Farmington hands let out a yell.

Buchanan held back. Breathing hard, Hal came again. Buchanan was content to ward off the shrewd blows. One got through, striking him on the jaw. He did not blink. Immediately he saw concern in Hal's expression. It had been a good punch, accepted with no effect. Hal began a retreat. Buchanan followed, again struck for the body. This time he hit the young man in the belly.

Hal doubled over. Buchanan cuffed him and he spun around and went headlong in the direction of his corner.

"Time!" Now Judson was beside himself. He jumped down from the carriage. He came rushing to his son. He spoke with terrible bitterness. "So you are the champion of Harvard College! No one can beat you with his fists. Is this the way you prove yourself? You are a dolt! Fight the man! Show him how good you are!"

Buchanan said to Rafe. "The roof's goin' to fall in."

The only response from Connors was a catch of the breath, a whispered prayer. "God give me strength."

Buchanan said, "Don't call on strangers when neighbors are near, Rafe."

Farmington was slapping at his son. Hal was trying hard to catch his breath and avoid the rage of his father. Buchanan felt a fleeting pity for the young man. The other Farmington men were gathering in, coming closer. Buchanan looked at Patricia Ann and spoke.

"Reckon this has gone far enough. I got no notion to cripple the boy for life."

Judson Farmington straightened. "You'll fight him to a finish. You'll do it now, do you hear? I call time!"

He shoved Hal out to center ring. Buchanan waited. Hal lifted his hands. He was still hurting from the body blow. Buchanan moved right, then left, keeping everyone in sight except the women against the building.

Hal tried to move right. Buchanan hooked with the left. His huge fist broke through Hal's guard, smashed against the side of his head.

The younger Farmington went down like a poled ox. His father screamed in rage and lifted the rifle. Buchanan never stopped for forward motion. He clipped Judson Farmington on the chin.

The old man fell across the body of his son. Buchanan knelt behind the two bodies and produced his little hideout gun.

"Everybody hold it," he said calmly. "You're covered every whichaway."

He had seen Patricia Ann make her move. She had the shotgun on the black man and Symes. Brogan was close enough to be under Buchanan's muzzle. Rafe Connors reached beneath his shirt and came out with an old, flat Navy Colt. And Consuela stopped twisting her apron and from it showed Molly's .38.

Nobody stirred for a long moment. Then Brogan stood up and said, "I'll be a money's damn uncle."

"You'll be a dead monkey if you don't pile these carcasses in the carriage and take off." Buchanan motioned to the black man in the background. "You, there. Come and give him a hand."

Joe Glass came reluctantly. His gun was tied low on his flank. He was boiling with the desire to get a shot at the man who had wounded him. Buchanan watched his every move. Symes stood, irresolute, eyeballs showing white as he estimated the damage Patricia Ann's shotgun could do to him.

Buchanan said, "You, there, round up the horses. And you be real careful like, too."

"I'm careful," muttered Symes. He went to where the horses waited. Buchanan whistled and Nightshade came trotting. Patricia Ann gently pushed the roan so that it did not walk into the line of fire should anyone grow brave and reckless. Buchanan nudged the two horses toward the barn.

The three henchmen were picking up the Farmingtons. It was a task to get them into the buggy, Glass managing with one arm. Brogan cursed under his breath.

Buchanan said, "Watch your language, gunny. There's ladies present."

Brogan paused a moment in his effort. "If you say so, Buchanan. I ain't buckin' a case like this."

"You keep buckin' us and you'll get throwed good and long and hard," Buchanan advised him. "You got a crazy boss, there. Was I you, I'd take a long ride south."

"Was you me, you'd do your job," said the brash cowboy. "You're one hell of a big man—beggin' your pardon, ladies—but I seen the big ones go down."

Buchanan shrugged. "You pays your money and you takes your chances."

They propped the groggy father and son into the carriage. Buchanan picked up the Remington sporting rifle. He hefted it. "This the old man's favorite?"

Brogan said, "That's the one he can shoot with. Got to say he shoots good, too."

Buchanan took the bullet from the scene of the massacre from his pocket. He made a comparison, shook his head. "Can't prove a thing. But I got notions. You might tell him that."

Brogan said, "He knows you got notions. He's got a heap of his own."

"Best to take him away before he wakes up and plumb explodes," Buchanan suggested.

He was watching the black man. The carriage pulled away with the Farmingtons lolling against each. Symes was waiting with the horses. Glass began walking toward him, then spun and crouched.

"Buchanan!" he said.

Buchanan swung around, threw Farmington's rifle. He ducked, knelt with the deadly little derringer ready.

The butt of the rifle caught Glass and spun him. When he could see straight again, Buchanan, Rafe, Consuela and Patricia Ann all had their guns pointed at him.

Buchanan said, "That was a damfool play, mister. It could've got you much worse than a scratch on your shoulder. Better save it 'til next time."

"Next time I'll have you in my sights afore you can play your tricks," said Glass. "Then good-bye big man, good-bye!"

"Uh-huh," said Buchanan wearily. "You and all them others and plenty more people. Good-bye, for now."

Glass picked up Farmington's gun, very carefully, then

plodded to his horse and mounted. Symes led Brogan's mount. They rode without looking back. They probably half expected a bullet in the back for each, Buchanan thought. They were a bad bunch, as bad as they came in this part of Texas.

Rafe brought his shirt to him. Patricia Ann still held the shotgun but she was staring at Buchanan. He donned the shirt, somewhat self-conscious. Molly was patting Consuela, telling her how brave she had been.

Patricia Ann said, "Buchanan, you sure got a body on you like a real giant."

He felt himself flushing. "Girls ain't supposed to be gawkin' at a fella."

"I ain't gawkin'. I'm plumb admirin'," she told him.

Her mother swung around and called, "Put up that greener and take care of your horse, Patricia Ann. Then come in and help with the supper. I swear, there's no end to your foolishment."

The girl went into the stable. As she passed Buchanan she gave him a huge wink and a warm smile.

Rafe said under his breath, "She's gone head-over-heels. Never did see her pay attention to any man."

"You feelin' your oats?" Buchanan asked testily.

"Nope. Just observin' what I observe," Rafe said. "She's some kind of a woman, too."

"Just a child."

Rafe hooted. "You ain't blind, Tom Buchanan. Don't tell me."

"You better mend your hoe handle." Buchanan picked up his vest. His gunbelt was in the dirt alongside the carriage where he had seen it fall while the Farmingtons were being shoved into the carriage. He would have to clean it and see to the Colt. He felt unbalanced, a bit. He could not pretend to ignore the girl. Maybe he didn't want to, he told himself. Maybe he was a damn fool.

Judson Farmington lay in the canopied bed he had brought from Boston. The bedroom on the second floor of the house was huge. They were all gathered there, a Mexican woman hovering, dampening the bandage around the head of the old man. Hal, his face swollen, sat in a deep chair, sulking, all his manhood drained.

The eyes of the old man gleamed from deep caverns. "So. You met the legend and you were beaten, eh?"

"We were all beaten," said Hal in a monotone. "Women, a cripple and a legend. They beat us all."

Brogan spoke for the trio comprising himself, Glass and Symes, all standing, all with thoughts of their own. "T'wasn't only Buchanan. That gal with the blunderbuss, she'd of blown Symes to bits given half a chance."

"Men against a crowd like that." Judson Farmington did not rail at them this time. "It is not in the realm of reason."

"It happened," Brogan pointed out.

Judson Farmington said, half to himself, "Yet I cannot fault any of you."

They stared in disbelief. This was not the loud, irascible tyrant they had known. Hal drained the glass of whiskey he was holding and the serving girl took it and refilled it from a decanter.

Judson said, "Whiskey for all of them." He tried to prop himself up on the pillows and failed. His son went to his aid and Judson looked up at him. "You tried. You were brave. You stood up to the legend."

Hal choked, then said, "Thank you, Father."

"They will be destroyed. All of them." The voice was cold now, without bombast, deadly.

Brogan said, " 'Scuse me, boss, but this is gonna get out and around. In this country news travels."

"Of course."

"So that idea of burnin' them out, cuttin' 'em down, that won't work."

"Of course it won't. It was a threat. No matter how accidental it may be made to seem, we could not survive."

"That's right," said Brogan. "People wouldn't hold still for it, not now."

"And we have forgotten our primary objective. The man Buchanan has thrown us off the real mission."

"The treasure," said Hal. He sipped the whiskey. His head throbbed. "Millions, enough for us all."

"Brogan, Glass, Symes, can you handle our other men? Control them?"

"They ain't nothin' but waddies," Brogan said. "We can keep 'em where they belong."

"I promise you enough shares to make you rich," Judson told them. "You will be able to leave the country and start over."

"Shoot!" said Brogan. "With that kind of money we can start a spread of our own. Bigger men than us have done worse and stayed right here in the West."

"Whatever your desire." Judson fixed them with unwavering gaze. "Think about it. You may go now."

The three gunslingers departed. The old man waited until they were out of the house, then said to his son, "Now they are truly bound to us. Glass wants to kill Buchanan. The others want money. They will be loyal."

"The treasure," Hal said. "What do you think, sir?"

"I have seen Buchanan in action. You are a good fighter, son. Very good. Yet he handled you as though you were a child. Do you think that man will fail at anything he endeavors?"

Hal winced, then nodded. "Yes, sir. I see what you mean. He is a brute."

"Would you face him with a gun?"

"I would, sir." He made a quick motion and the gun was in his hand. "I am very quick, sir."

"Well, do not try it upon Buchanan. He is quicker. I saw him today. He is unbelievable. It will take time and thought to get the better of him."

"But first—let him lead us to the treasure. Is that what you have in mind?"

"Precisely." Judson closed his eyes and leaned back his head. "I will think about it. Have the men keep an eye on Buchanan as before. And . . . I was proud of you, son. For once I was truly proud of you."

Hal said, "Thank you, sir." He went out of the room. He took the whiskey with him. In his own bedchamber he sat down. He found that he was trembling.

It was very strange. His father's praise had not made him feel warm. This new stance bewildered him—it was not Judson Farmington. There must be something behind it, some deep meaning. He could, he thought, never, never believe in his father. Too much dirty water had run under their bridges.

And there was the girl. She had been so quick and brave, her eyes had shone like stars. His father had spoken ill of her. Hal could never have the girl while his father lived—or while Buchanan lived. Not for a little while, not at all. He put the whiskey down and rose to face the pier glass mirror, another relic of Boston days. He regarded himself full length, and struck an intimidating stance.

He flashed out the gun. Again and again he made his move. It seemed to him that nobody could stand up against the speed of his underarm draw.

He returned to the whiskey. Down the hall his father was loudly cursing the serving woman. Listening to that harsh, cold voice, he repeated to himself that there could never be peace or understanding between Judson and himself.

He tried to concentrate, thinking desperate thoughts, attempting to make plans. His father had shown signs of mania that day. Hal had not come completely ignorant from Harvard. He recognized derangement, loss of balance in the old man's mind.

If only they could have found the treasure, shared it properly with the Cuestas. If only the girl . . . The whiskey drained low in the bottle until finally he slept with his dreams.

6

Buchanan tiptoed into the kitchen, hoping not to disturb anyone. The odor of bacon and eggs assailed his nostrils.

He said, "Consuela, how do you manage it?"

She dimpled at him. She seemed prettier this morning. She held her head high as she winked. "I am *simpático*, no?"

"*Simpático*," he repeated. "You sure speak good, girl."

"I am taught by Señora," she said proudly. "I have the dictionary. When we find the treasure I will go to school, no?"

"You were very brave yesterday."

"The señora forgot her pistol," she said simply. "I knew you would whip the boy. I was ready."

"You knew? How come you knew?" He sat down to a half-dozen eggs and a rasher of bacon.

She tapped her temple, still smiling. She poured coffee

and sat opposite with one between her brown hands. "I know."

"How long have you been here, on the ranch?"

She looked surprised. "I was born here. My father and his father and his father were born here."

"Uh-huh," said Buchanan. "Your father was with Benito?"

"But of course." She saddened. "My mother, she died soon after."

"Then you know all the stories about the treasure."

She nodded wisely. "All of them. Stories."

"But you have your own idea of where it is hidden?"

She hesitated for a long moment. She drank coffee, she looked past Buchanan to the window. Then she said in a voice almost inaudible, "The water."

Buchanan's eyes lit up. "The water. Yes. I been lookin' for a dried-up stream. Somethin' to do with water away back then."

She shook her head. "I think not."

"No?"

"It comes and goes, my thought." Again she tapped her temple. "It is never bright, how you say? Clear."

Buchanan said, "But you do get notions?"

"Yes. Notions." She shook her head, the light left her big, brown eyes. "It makes my head ache."

He went back to the food. When he had finished she took an apple pie from the oven and shyly placed it before him.

"A big fighter needs big food," she told him. "You ride today?"

"I ride to check on Jimson and Pecos."

Her smile returned. "Funny men."

"You think so?"

"Very funny. Not vaqueros, eh?"

"Uh-huh," said Buchanan. He put away the pie and arose, reaching for his Stetson. "You are a very smart young lady. I'll talk to you later, when your head does not hurt. Okay?"

"Sí, señor."

Consuela watched him walk out the door, and then she sat down and placed both hands tightly against her cheeks. Sometimes she was frightened by the thoughts that stirred within her head.

Buchanan rode through the brasada, following the trail. He saw several head of C-R cattle but made no attempt to chouse them to the gather. When he came to the place where the three boys were working, one of them was acting as cook, waiting on Bottles Jimson and Pecos Harder.

The latter two leaped to their feet when Nightshade pushed his head into the scene. Buchanan swung down. The three boys retired to the background and waited, as though expecting a pleasant show.

Buchanan picked up a tin cup and the boy acting as cook filled it without words. Bottles and Pecos moved nervously, fiddling with their plates.

"Sure you had enough breakfast?" Buchanan asked.

"We was kinda late gettin' started today," Bottles said. "Course, it ain't like we're makin' a real herd."

Buchanan looked at the scrubby pasture where the Cuesta cattle were being held. "Haven't brought in many since I was here last, I see."

"Like I said. None goin' up the trail this year."

"How about next year?" Buchanan did not raise his voice.

"Well, we ain't exactly figurin' on next year. We ain't been paid lately," said Pecos, popping his Adam's apple.

"You're just dreamin' of the Cuesta treasure, is that it? You came here because you heard tell of it. You're no cowmen whatsoever, right?"

"We worked for the biggest spreads in the West," objected Jimson. "Pecos here is a top wrangler."

Buchanan said, "Uh-huh. Well, then. Let's see you top my black horse here."

"Why, that's a broke saddle horse," said Pecos. "Ain't nothin' to settin' a broke horse. We got no bad ones around here right now or I'd show you a thing or two."

"Just show me on Nightshade," Buchanan purred. "Like to see how you handle a real horse."

Pecos ambled over to Nightshade's left. Buchanan whistled below his breath. Nightshade did a pirouette, placing Pecos on the wrong side.

Pecos said, "Whoa, now there, black hoss. Jist steady."

Nightshade pricked up his ears and turned to look at the alleged wrangler. Then he stood quite still until Pecos had come around and put a foot in the stirrup.

Then Nightshade stood straight on his hind legs. When he came down, Pecos had pitched headlong without ever touching his seat to the saddle. He landed on top of the cook's fire, rolled over and howled. He jumped up, beating at his pants with his hat.

Buchanan asked, "You want to try it, Jimson?"

"You got a trick horse there," said the ex-foreman sullenly. "What you want from us, Buchanan, anyway?"

"A little work. I passed some beef on my way. I want you to round it up. I want it pushed to grazin' on the C-R, nearer the house, you know the place. I want night guard. What few head we got, I want it protected until calvin' time. I want this place run right. I want the house repaired, the barn painted. I want a hell of a lot from you two saddle bums and these kids who seem willin' to work."

Pecos began, "I be damned. . . ."

Buchanan took out a pouch. "Fair's fair and right's right. Here's a month's pay for each and every one of you. Now I'm goin' to leave. Either you work—or you git. Because if I see you again and you ain't workin'—there'll be plain hell to pay."

One of the boys called, "Remember what we heard, Bottles. You know!"

Jimson accepted the money. "There was a rider passin' through. Said you had some trouble with the Farmingtons, said you handled 'em good. That suits me."

"The news even gets out here like you had a telegraph wire," said Buchanan. "I reckon the big fellas over yonder makin' the trail herd got wind of it?"

"That's where the rider was headin'," said Jimson.

"Uh-huh," said Buchanan. "It figures. Now you heed me. I'll be around awhile."

Jimson looked at the money. "Okay, Buchanan. And—about that Cuesta treasure?"

"Which brought you here, of course."

"Well . . . yeah, sure. But we ain't thieves."

"You're not? I just hope you'll be able to prove that to me. Because you been stealin' money from a widow and her daughter, pretendin' to be what you ain't." There was scorn in Buchanan's voice. "See you make it up to them."

He mounted and rode back the way he had come to the camp. He pulled up in the yard of the Cuesta ranch. Rafe was mending the rake handle. Consuela was at the pump, rinsing ladies' underwear. Each had a gun near at hand. Buchanan greeted them and went inside.

Molly Cuesta sat at the kitchen table. There was a ledger open before her. Buchanan removed his hat and sat opposite her.

She said, "It's come down to the last dollar, Tom."

"Forget it now, I got ideas."

"But the men must be paid."

"They're paid."

She shook her handsome head slowly at him. "Tom, you can't do that. We've nothin' to give you in return."

"Call it a loan to old friends."

She said, "You'll never get it back unless we find the treasure. And there's no chance of that."

"No chance?"

"Nobody's ever come close," she said bitterly. "If Benito was close—the Farmingtons would've found it. They were near enough."

Buchanan said, "I believe the Farmingtons killed Benito and his men. I can't prove it but I believe it. That don't cut any ice so far as the treasure's concerned."

"What do you mean?"

"Water. The whole thing turns to the water. Consuela remembers her grandfather's talk somewhat. Always water."

"I know. The wording on that old scrap. . . . But what water? Where? Maybe it's dried up years ago."

"That's what I thought," he said. "You people will be all right here for a while. Farmington'll think twice before he makes another try. I'll be ridin' to town."

"It's hopeless. Everybody's been all over the records until they're dog-eared."

"Uh-huh. But I'll be ridin' in. Give me a list of the supplies you need."

"No. You've done enough, payin' the men and all."

"Give me the list," he said gently. "I'll hitch up the wagon. Come on, Molly. Let a friend help."

Patricia Ann came into the kitchen. "Ma. Please. Let him help. We can't go on without him."

"You too?" Molly sighed. "I thought you had too much pride."

"I got pride," said the girl. "I also got some common sense. I see where we either find the treasure or go down the hole. And I aim to let Buchanan help me as much as he can."

"Patricia Ann! You're bein' bold as a hussy."

"Maybe I am a hussy. I know this much: If somethin' don't happen for us soon, I'll be workin' a saloon in some place bigger'n Yaqui!"

Molly opened her mouth, closed it. Then she took a slip of paper from the pages of the ledger and slid it toward Buchanan. "Charity. I never thought I'd see the day when we accepted charity."

"A loan." Buchanan corrected her, pocketing the list. "I'll be back before dark. And—believe me, I have got a notion. No proof nor nothin'. But a notion."

He went out and Rafe helped him harness a team from the stable, docile harness stock. The lame man was smiling as he worked.

"Feel better now?" Buchanan asked him.

"You know how I feel."

"I don't expect trouble from the Farmingtons. But that black man, he may be gunnin' for me."

"Yeah. I could see the hate in him."

"Keep your eye on the house and keep your gun handy at all times," said Buchanan.

"It's you they'll be after."

"I got no doubt they're watchin' right now." Buchanan put his rifle beneath the seat of the wagon. "It's a time to be ready for anything. Judson's goin' to be thinkin' real hard how to get back at us. The boy, I don't know about him. I didn't hurt him too much. He may jump any old way."

Rafe said, "He and his old man are different. But each has got poison in him. You mind that."

"I mind 'em all. Watch close, now. You want anything from town?"

"Somethin' I ain't touched in years."

"Uh-huh," said Buchanan. "Monongahela or Old Crow?"

"I remember we drank Monongahela down by the Border."

"We'll drink it again," Buchanan promised.

He drove off on the road to Yaqui.

The town was still quiet as Buchanan drove down the main street, and backed the wagon to the loading platform of the general store. Yet there were eyes behind windows and there were open doors where figures lurked. There was an aura which he did not like, a sense of dire events forthcoming.

A woman customer deserted the store. Inside it was redolent of all the mixed smells of others of its kind. A dark-skinned boy was piling canned peaches upon a shelf. The owner, whose name was Hanson, was a thin man with thin features and wispy hair. He had protruding large, floppy ears.

Buchanan put the list he had brought from the ranch upon the counter. He picked up a stubby pencil and began adding items.

Hanson asked, "That the Cuesta wagon?"

"Uh-huh." Buchanan added two rashers of bacon and an extra bag of flour.

"Cash only," said Hanson.

Buchanan looked at him. "Just before roundup and you're askin' cash?"

"On the barrel head. This ain't no charity house."

"You make it sound like you don't want the Cuesta business," mused Buchanan.

"No how." Hanson was evidently a man of few words.

Buchanan added a few more items, including a case of the newly arrived canned peaches. He took out his pouch and placed several gold pieces on the bar. "I'll be totin' this up and lookin' for my change." He paused. "You are honest, ain't you?"

Hanson choked. Then he said, his eyes on the money, "Yup."

"Then be careful. My 'rithmetic is real good."

Hanson put his hand on the coins, stacked them. "Advice."

"Worth what it costs. Nothin'." Buchanan helped himself from the cracker barrel.

"You be careful."

Buchanan nodded. "Uh-huh. Anything partic'lar in that warnin'?"

"McGee." Hanson swept the coins into a drawer.

"Uh-huh," Buchanan repeated. "Thanks. See you later."

He was walking out the door when Hanson called, "Courthouse."

Buchanan walked down the street eating the crackers. He passed the marshal's office and saw the *Closed* sign again. He went to the courthouse. He was about to enter when the sound of gunfire rattled his eardrums. It came from within the building.

He burst through the door. McGee, the tall saloon keeper, pointed a rifle at him. Buchanan tossed the remaining crackers at the man, dropped to one knee, drew his Colt and fired, all in one flowing motion.

McGee's gun went off. The bullet nicked Buchanan's shirt sleeve. The saloonkeeper fell to the terrazzo floor of the courthouse. Blood streamed from a hole in his chest.

Mrs. Bascomb came from behind a filing cabinet, white-faced, tears streaming down her cheeks. "The doctor!" she cried. She ran out of the building.

The sound of coughing took Buchanan posthaste to the rear of the high-ceilinged room. Rusty Wallace lay on his side. There was a hole in his left arm. His gun lay beside him.

Buchanan asked, "McGee?"

"He jumped me as I was lookin' at an old map," breathed Wallace. "I . . . I think . . . river . . . I think . . ."

His eyes closed. Buchanan felt his pulse. He picked up the surprisingly light form and carried the marshal to the door. Mrs. Bascomb was coming in, followed by a small Mexican in black garments.

She said, "Dr. Gonzales. This is Buchanan."

The doctor nodded, looked a moment at the prone McGee. "He can wait, I think. For the undertaker, no?"

"I would expect so. He fired at me," Buchanan replied. "Where do you want my friend, here?"

"My office is nearby. Since you carry him so easily. Thank you."

It was a clean, airy office. The little doctor was quick and efficient. Buchanan, who had been attended to by many, felt that this one knew his business. He drew Mrs. Bascomb aside.

"Want to tell me about it?"

"Is he—is the marshal going to die?"

"Not from that wound," Buchanan assured her.

"But he is so weak. He had been in bed when McGee came roaring in about a map he said the marshal and I had been keeping from him."

"So that's how McGee got him. Rusty was slowed down."

"McGee was drunk. He was threatening me or anyone who stood between him and the map."

"What map?"

"I don't know," she said agonizedly. "I'd have given it to him had I known and Rusty . . . the marshal . . . would not have come to my rescue. I was frightened, I screamed. And he came through the door. . . . And McGee shot him before he could get his gun up and ready."

"Uh-huh." Buchanan could visualize it all. Rusty would gladly risk his life for the widow who had been taking care of him when he was ill. "Tell me, any of the Farmington crowd been in here today?"

"I don't think so," she said slowly. "But McGee often rides out to the ranch."

Dr. Gonzales was washing up. He was grave when he spoke to them. "Marshal Wallace has been ill, you know."

"Comsumption?"

"That's correct. He should have left town. . . . Well, he will be weak for some time. His disease has progressed too far. I cannot say when he will be up and around again."

"Can you take care of him?" Buchanan asked the widow.

"I can. And I will."

"Can you handle his gun?"

She gasped. "I . . . I'm a town woman. I . . . I don't know."

"I'll give you a lesson," Buchanan told her. "One more question. Is there a map in the courthouse over a hundred years old?"

"Why . . . yes. There is one. It's a curiosity piece. No one ever asks to see it."

Dr. Gonzales said, "I have seen it."

"Yes. And then I forgot we had it."

Buchanan asked, "Where is it kept?"

"In my desk," she replied. "In the middle drawer."

Dr. Gonzales said, "I could show you, sir."

"Then do so, right now," said Buchanan. An idea was forming in his mind. He walked so fast that the shorter man had trouble keeping up with him.

The middle drawer of Mrs. Bascomb's desk was locked. Buchanan shrugged and used the heavy blade of his knife. The map lay, unfolded, a crude drawing by some long gone map maker.

Dr. Gonzales said, "The Cuesta treasure, is it not?"

"It is." Buchanan shook his head. "Not that I know anything about its whereabouts."

"Too many people have dug and died." The doctor shook his head. "Do you believe in curses, sir?"

"Not any," said Buchanan. "I believe in people."

Dr. Gonzales looked hard at him, then his face softened. "The marshal, Mrs. Bascomb, they said you were a good man. I have no interest in treasure. But Señora Cuesta and the girl, they are people."

"Exactly," said Buchanan. "I'm takin' this map along. For them."

"I believe you."

Buchanan took off his vest and pulled up his shirt. He found a ball of twine and bound the map to his body. He rearranged his clothing. He said, "I'll be responsible to any law that might show up. Meantime I got supplies to run out to the C-R. Take care of Rusty. I'll foot the bill."

"For him and for you, sir, there will be no charge." The doctor bowed. "That will be my small contribution."

"As you wish." He shook the hand of the proud little man.

The purchases were already in the wagon. People had not come out of hiding to see what had happened in the street. Hanson counted out change, gave Buchanan the bill of lading. Buchanan studied it for a minute.

Hanson said, "No more McGee?"

"Uh-huh," answered Buchanan.

"A bad man."

"A dead man."

"Dead or alive—bad."

"I see you're a man of reality." Buchanan tucked away the bill. "Your figurin' is good, too. But you didn't charge me for the crackers."

"You eat 'em all?"

"They saved my life." Buchanan put down a silver dollar from the change. "About all it's worth, maybe."

Hanson put the dollar in the drawer. "You set the price."

"I sure do like a man gets right to the point." Buchanan grinned and went outside and climbed onto the seat of the wagon, careful not to wrinkle the map. Hanson, his arms folded beneath the high-waisted apron of his craft, watched him drive away.

A dark-skinned youth skinned out the back door and loped away, running with the ease and grace of an Indian. He was headed in the direction of the Farmington ranch.

Molly Cuesta watched Rafe, Patricia Ann and Buchanan unload the wagon. She bit her lip as the supplies were put away. Rafe was a new man, jovial, moving with greater ease than he had hitherto shown.

Buchanan went into the house. He removed his vest and produced the old, crude map from beneath his shirt. Molly sat behind her desk and watched. When she spoke her voice was hard.

"I got to talk to you, Tom."

He was turning the map to the light, poring over it. "Uh-huh. There's somethin' here if I can only think it out."

She said, "I can't pay you for the supplies. And I know Hanson wouldn't put it on my bill."

Buchanan looked up. "It's a loan. I got it all marked down. See?" He showed her the bill. "Hanson's an honest man. There's no problem here."

She said, "Furthermore, there's Patricia Ann."

"A great gal." Buchanan returned to the map.

"You think so?"

"I know so."

"How good is she?"

He scowled, "That's a whale of a question, Molly. I got no answer for that."

"She's in love with you."

"That's a lot of nonsense," he retorted. "We've all been through a few things together. Naturally, since we didn't any of us get killed, she thinks I'm somebody. Well, I ain't."

"That's not the point. Patricia Ann won't hold anything back. That's not her nature."

Buchanan mused, "Now, where could they put that loot? They couldn't bury it. They couldn't dump it in the river. But the parchment, it says definitely 'water'! So what water? Where in water? Farmington must have a glimmer, he ain't nohow stupid."

"Tom Buchanan, you listen to me," she cried.

"I'm listenin'," he replied mildly. "I just ain't payin' much attention."

She flushed. "I know how you are with women."

"You accusin' me of playin' funny games?" he grinned at her.

"No. But I am worried about my daughter. She's a wild young fool in many ways."

"So was I." He sighed. "Yep. I mind goin' up the trail as a boy: Dodge City, whooeee!" He glared at her. "You think I haven't growed up? You think I'm just an old fool?"

"You're in your thirties. That ain't old," she said grimly. "Too old for Patricia Ann, though. You know you ain't the marryin' kind."

He softened. "You're right, Molly. Me, I'm married to the country. Mostly I'm a loner. Fishin', huntin', visitin' with friends. And Molly—you're my friend."

There was silence in the room. Buchanan did not remove his gaze from the woman.

Finally she said, "Oh, Tom! Lemme look at that damn map."

They were studying it when Consuela announced supper. They went in together, then Buchanan returned to the office, opened the safe and put the map inside.

Patricia Ann was radiant. There was ham and beans and plenty of vegetables and corn bread. There was a big peach pie, which Consuela served.

The Mexican girl had been silent amid the merriment. Buchanan, noticing this, tried to draw her into the conversation, praising her for her bravery and quick thinking, asking her questions about herself.

She replied at length, "I have been thinking. About when I was a small child."

"Yes?" Buchanan was aware of her serious mien. "You want to talk about it?"

She said hesitantly, "I have good English, no?"

"Yes. You speak better'n most of us."

She said, "There is a word my grandmama used. She spoke of the treasure. She said 'grotto.' What is it, a grotto?"

Buchanan frowned. "Got a dictionary around here?"

"In the office," Molly told him.

"I ain't quite certain," he said. "Let's take a look. Grotto? I heard it someplace. Like a cave?"

The big dictionary was in the office. They went to it upon its high, wooden stand. Buchanan leafed the pages. He read, " 'Grotto, a cave or cavern.' But they've rooted into every cave and cavern in this part of the country."

In a small voice, Consuela repeated, "Grotto."

"Her grandmother spoke little English," Molly said. "Could she have meant something else?"

Buchanan was reading on, " 'A subterranean passage.' Uh-huh. Let's look up subterranean."

"Grotto," repeated Consuela as a litany.

" 'Beneath the surface of the earth,' " muttered Buchanan. "Can't be. Beneath the surface . . . But the parchment says water. Beneath the surface . . . a cavern . . . beneath the water?"

There was a clap of thunder, a bolt of lightning. A sudden Texas rain beat against the window. Buchanan put his hand to his head.

"The horses!" cried Patricia Ann. Rafe joined her and they ran for slickers, then to the corral.

Molly said to the Mexican girl. "Sit down. You look like you seen a ghost."

Consuela, still speaking in a low monotone, said, "Grotto . . . Water . . . My grandmama . . . *Sí*, señora. Beneath the water as Señor Buchanan says."

He went to the safe. He took out the map, matched it against the modern map of the C-R Ranch. Molly lit a lamp and brought it close. Consuela seemed in a trance, sitting bolt upright on a chair. Outdoors the storm increased in violence.

Buchanan said, "I kept thinkin' about rivers changin' their course. This here river runs through rock, down from the hills. It didn't change. It takes more'n a hundred years to wear away Texas granite."

"Then they could have put it in the river. "But where?" Molly shook her head. "And wouldn't the river carry it away, scatter it?"

"But not a bit of it has been found," Buchanan said. "We got to look for an underwater cave, blocked by now, no doubt, by rock carried downstream."

"Grotto," came the monotone from Consuela. "Rock."

Molly said, "But Tom! It's a damn long stream."

"It's a damn big treasure," said Buchanan.

"The Farmingtons will be watching our every move."

"Uh-huh," he agreed. His mind was working again along practical lines. "You think you can trust Jimson and Pecos?"

"No."

"But they've never stolen anything. Or acted in any way to make you think they'd go against you?"

"Well, no."

"I think we need them. I think we might put the fear of God in them—and offer them a bribe if we find the treasure."

Molly said, "If you think so."

"The storm will probably cause the stream to overflow. Still, I want to start lookin' tomorrow. I kinda got a hunch. I know hunches ain't worth much. But they're worth a shot."

She said, "Molly is the best swimmer in Texas."

"Uh-huh. And Rafe came up with an idea." Buchanan sat back. He looked at the maps. He tried to visualize what might have happened when the Indians attacked the Cuesta expedition, and what happened when it became obvious there were too many of them to fight. "I don't think Benito was on the right track, do you?"

"He said nothing about water, the river," Molly replied. "He was going upstream, though. I just don't know, Tom."

He stared long and hard at the maps. If the topography had not altered measurably in this part of the land not covered by the brasada, the Indians would have attacked at a spot where they could lie in ambush. He put his finger on one spot, then another. The storm whirled against the old house.

Consuela said, "My grandmama was not there. But someone told her about a grotto. I do not know who it could have been."

"It don't matter," Buchanan told her gently. "You've given us a start, Consuela."

"You think so?" asked Molly. Her hopes had been dashed too often; she was not confident.

"I know it's worth a chance. Any little old clue is worth followin'," he told her.

They heard the voices of Patricia Ann and Rafe in the kitchen. Buchanan put the maps back in the safe. Molly twirled the combination. They all sat around the kitchen table.

Buchanan said, "Rafe, I want two things. I want two more of those contraptions you built for the blue horse. I want 'em big enough and safe enough to carry ammunition as well as guns. And when you got them done, I want you to take a note to Jimson and Pecos to bring them in."

"They ain't any use where they are now, for a fact," said Rafe.

"Can you do it before noon tomorrow?"

"I can make the contraptions. Then I can ride."

"Take your guns."

"Wouldn't be without 'em," said Rafe.

"The rest of you best go to bed. If the storm lets up we got work tomorrow."

Patricia Ann asked, "You know somethin', don't you, Tom?"

"Maybe."

"You'll find it," she said exultantly. "I know you'll find it and set us all free."

She threw her arms around him and kissed him soundly, fully upon the mouth. Then she fled up the stairs on her long, shapely legs, her hips swinging at every step.

Molly looked hard at Buchanan. He coughed.

He said, "She's not a little girl. You're right about that, Molly."

"See you remember." But she smiled and a bit of hope showed in her. "Whatever happens, I know you will."

"Uh-huh," said Buchanan. But he could not completely subdue a certain feeling that had stolen into him.

Judson Farmington was out of bed, seated beside a roaring fire downstairs in the ranch house. Hal sat in his usual place. Brogan came to the doorway and said, "I'm soaked. I give the breed kid the dollar. He's sleepin' in the barn."

"You can go to bed now," said Judson. "Tomorrow you three get onto Buchanan and never let him out of your sight."

Brogan nodded and departed. The two men stared into the fire. The whiskey decanter was between them.

Judson said, "There's something about that old map."

"You have a copy."

"I know. But McGee got onto something. I wonder how? Too damn bad he's dead."

"He took our money. He was a crook."

"Of course. People who accept bribes are generally dishonest." Judson's voice again was becoming acid when he spoke to his son. "You had better learn that lesson."

"That's why Buchanan is so dangerous, isn't it? Because nothing can deter him from aiding his friends."

"Because he's one of those fools who believe in the mythical code of the frontier," Judson said. "They are doomed. Civilization will soon make them truly legendary. And stone dead in their graves."

"In the meantime?"

"In the meantime, my boy, we do not know this land as does Buchanan—and the women—and the lame man. In Boston we could reconstruct events. Here, we can only use the knowledge of others. We have been wrong in trying first to destroy Buchanan. It is evident the girl is not for marrying. Not you, in any case."

Hal winced. "Yes, sir, it would so seem."

"Therefore we watch. We allow them to do what they can to locate the Cuesta treasure."

"And then?"

"We wipe them out. We have no law now that Wallace

is bedded down. I doubt he will ever recover. His lungs are gone. He now has a bullet wound, thanks to McGee. We need only to destroy Buchanan and the Cuestas— and depart under cover of night." He beamed as though he had just planned a Christmas party for all concerned.

"And how do we wipe them out?"

"With the aid of Brogan, Symes and Glass," said his father calmly. "It may be necessary to pay them off, meantime watching them lest they turn upon us." He closed his eyes for a moment, then went on. "You are quick with the gun. Perhaps you had better be ready to dispose of them. I will, of course, be with you. If we take them by surprise, we can certainly vanquish them."

"Yes, sir." He quaked at the thought but was careful not to show his unease. "And the girl?"

"Whatever happens—will happen. You want her. You cannot have her excepting by force. And so far as I can determine, she might be too much for you in any case."

"I do not want her by force," said Hal stiffly. "I do not consider that a pleasure."

"No. There is certainly a soft spot in you. Maybe that is why you could not whip Buchanan."

Hal swallowed hard, then managed to say quietly, "Brogan tells me that no one has ever beaten Buchanan with his fists. The scars he wears are all from bullets or arrows or knives thrown at him from a distance. He is, as you have said yourself, a living legend."

"And you are not. Nor ever will be." Judson poured whiskey into his glass. "However, once the Cuesta treasure is ours and we are back safely in civilization, no doubt we can find you an acquiescent lady. You will soon forget your Texas slut."

Hal choked. "If you'll excuse me, I think I'll retire. Good night, Father."

"Good night, son." Judson looked onto the fire, sipping his whiskey. He did not see the mottled rage that Hal took with him to his bed chamber.

Rusty Wallace lay in his bed in the house belonging to Mrs. Bascomb. His eyes were open but he was so still that she was frightened, seated at his side.

"Lily?" His voice was less than a whisper.

"Don't talk," she begged.

"Got to . . . McGee . . . What did he want?"

"The old map."

"Did he . . . get it?"

"Buchanan shot him."

"Dead?"

She nodded. "Please don't talk. Dr. Gonzales says it'll start you coughing again."

"The . . . map?"

"I gave it to Buchanan."

He sighed and managed to nod his head. "The treasure . . . It's there . . . some place."

She said, "McGee probably learned something spying on the Farmingtons. They had old maps from libraries in the East, you remember? Now McGee was born and raised in this country. He might have figured something. The Farmingtons, not being from hereabouts, they wouldn't have the knowledge of the terrain that McGee had."

"Buchanan . . . He might figure . . . He's smart. . . ." He moved a hand. "But they'll be watchin' him. . . . I oughta . . . "

"You cannot move for at least a week."

"There's no law . . . in Yaqui."

"Please, Rusty."

He reached out a few more inches and she took his hand. "What's the difference . . . ?"

"You must lie still. Dr. Gonzales is coming in every day. Maybe this rest will . . . help you."

He smiled faintly, "Nothin's gonna help me. . . . But Buchanan . . . he's an honest man. . . . Depend on him."

"Please don't talk."

He closed his eyes again. He lay thinking of his daughter and her children. He thought of Buchanan down on the Border in the old days. He remembered how they had fought together with the guns flashing and the outlaws going down and Buchanan laughing. If there was a chance, any chance, it would depend upon Buchanan. . . .

The woman watched him, tears in her eyes. She had loved him for years. His illness had saddened her from the start. Now that it was so serious, she had little hope of his survival. She had seen her husband die of the same disease; she knew all the symptoms. She gently released his hand so that she could kneel. She prayed.

Outdoors the rain pelted down. She wondered if her plea could get through to heaven.

7

In the morning it still stormed. At noon Rafe returned with Jimson and Pecos Harder, all soaking wet. Buchanan gathered them in the bunkhouse, where a fire burned to dry their clothing. They poked curiously at the waterproof contraptions that Rafe had built, while Rafe, worthy and sleepless, bundled himself into clean long johns and snuggled onto a bed.

Buchanan said, "Seems to me you men once allowed as how you ain't scared of much."

"That goes," said Jimson. Pecos shuffled his feet and nodded agreement.

"Now you know—and I know—you ain't real good cattlemen."

Jimson squirmed, then agreed. "That's right."

"Been miners?"

"Been just about everything. Exceptin' we never rode the hoot-owl trail."

"I believe you," said Buchanan. "But you did come here with some notions about the Cuesta treasure."

"That's right," said Jimson. "How about you?"

"I work for Señora Cuesta," Buchanan pointed out. "So do y'all. You want to stay on the job and maybe get a share if we find the treasure?"

"You got some ideas about it?"

"Maybe. Thing is, can you take orders?"

Jimson said, "We was in the cavalry together."

"Honorable discharges?"

"In my saddlebags." He did not resent the question. Many a soldier had deserted the hard duty on the frontier.

"Uh-huh," said Buchanan. "I'm takin' your word."

Pecos spoke for the first time. "They got some bad people over yonder."

"But you're not scared," Buchanan reminded him.

"Just figurin'," said Pecos.

Jimson added, "Like how do we stand?"

"It's a big fortune if we find it. How about a thousand apiece?"

They stared at him, then at one another. Then Jimson shook his head. "I'd ruther it'd be shares."

Buchanan shrugged. "Okay. You want to draw your pay now or later?"

"Hey! We didn't mean to quit!"

"Not quit. You're fired," said Buchanan.

"Now, you wait a minute." Jimson again looked at Pecos. They had been together so long, Buchanan thought, that they didn't need words to convey meaning to each other. It could be an advantage in a tight spot. Jimson went on, "If one of us gets hurt?"

"You'll be taken care of."

"Or buried," said Pecos.

"That, too. You fought Indians for eight dollars a month," Buchanan told them.

Jimson said, "A thousand. And that's for each."

"If we live," said Pecos.

Buchanan said, "That's the deal. And . . . you take orders. From me."

Again they exchanged glances. Then Jimson said, "It's a deal, Buchanan."

"Okay. Now, you say you done some minin'. All kinds?"

"Just about."

"You know how to handle a pick and shovel?"

Jimson made a wry face. "Not willingly."

"Think of the thousand dollars apiece. You go to town and pick up some tools. Let it be thought you've quit and are lookin' for the treasure. You go up the river a half mile or so and you start diggin' around."

"You think the treasure is there?"

"I think the Farmingtons'll have to split their forces to spy on you and me and the rest of us. They got three men and the two of them. Father and son. I don't reckon much on them."

"They're meaner'n a wounded rattlesnake."

"But they don't know the country. And they think you do and that I do. So they'll be wonderin' and that's the way I want to keep them."

"Is that all we got to do?"

"That's all so far. Unless a fight starts."

Jimson nodded. "We wouldn't run from a fight. On t'other hand we ain't pickin' one with Brogan and them."

Pecos added hastily, "Not that we're scared, it just wouldn't be healthy."

Buchanan took out his money bag, which was growing

lighter every day. He handed coins to Jimson and said, "Okay. Get goin'."

"In this here rain?"

"It'll make people think you're real anxious," Buchanan assured them.

Dubiously, they donned their ponchos and left the bunkhouse. Rafe opened one eye.

"You reckon you can trust 'em?"

"No," said Buchanan. "But we got to take chances. Otherwise we'd have to cold wipe out the Farmingtons and their gunners. And you know we ain't in that business."

"Sooner or later," said Rafe sleepily. In a moment he was snoring.

Buchanan ran to the house. The storm was lessening but the river and the dam would be swollen tomorrow. He went to his room and took out a pair of Levi's and, emulating Patricia Ann, cut them off short. He carefully assembled .44 caliber ammunition that would fit either his short gun or the rifle. He padded downstairs and went into the kitchen. Consuela was putting food into sacks. Patricia Ann was examining the .38. Molly watched it all, worrying.

"You shouldn't go out in this storm. Lightning could strike you. And around water and trees! It's loco."

Buchanan said, "They won't be watchin' today. Also, since they got some kind of spy in town, I'm givin' 'em something to think about." He told of his orders to Jimson and Pecos.

"Just our luck they'll dig up the treasure," Molly said. "And I got to set here with Rafe and Consuela and wait it all out."

"You want to do somethin'?" asked Buchanan.

"Of course I do."

"You stay here. Keep busy. Watch for anyone scoutin' around. Keep your rifle handy. Also a shotgun. If anybody tries to break in—shoot 'em."

"You think they'll try that again?"

"They'll be real busy tryin' anything that comes into their heads," Buchanan assured her.

"I can't go with you and Patricia Ann?"

"It wouldn't help."

"But you could be drowned. And . . . Tom?"

"Uh-huh."

"You look awful silly with your hairy legs stickin' outa them cutdown pants."

Buchanan said with dignity, "Silly is as silly does. Patricia Ann, are you ready?"

"I'm ready."

They went to the bunkhouse and took the waterproof contraptions while Rafe slept. They saddled Blue and Nightshade and attached the rather unwieldy paraphernalia. Nightshade objected and it took Buchanan a few moments to calm him down. Then they rode into the storm, heading for the dam where Patricia Ann swam so often in the sun. The rain beat down on them but they kept grimly on.

The day was black. Buchanan uncoiled two ropes. He attached one to the pommel of each saddle. He could barely distinguish Patricia Ann in the storm. She moved very close to him and even in the chill of the surroundings he could feel the warmth of her young flesh.

"Buchanan?"

"Uh-huh."

"I'm scared."

"Why, honey, this is the best time to be here, doin' what we got to do. Nobody's goin' to watch on an afternoon like this."

"The dark," she moaned. "I was always scared of the dark. Even when I was a baby."

He put a comforting arm around her. "You had the sand to come out here. So you ain't really scared."

She clung to him. "You think so?"

"I know so," It was getting too warm between them and he hastily went on. "We got work to do. Cold work. Has that Blue of yours ever worked cattle?"

"My Blue? In the brush, yes."

"He know your signal on a rope?"

"You mean like cuttin'? I never used him for that, fear he'd get hurt."

"Then it's goin' to be tougher. What we do, we go down below the surface with the rope's end, you see? Then we got to teach the horses to obey when we pull in one direction or the other."

"You really think they can learn that?"

"Nightshade can. He's smarter'n I am most of the time."

"It don't sound reasonable Blue could learn so quick."

Buchanan thought a minute. "So we'll try it. Dive down, then see that happens when you tug on the rope."

"It's so black. And cold, the water will be cold."

"You want me to go first?"

"No! Then I'd be alone . . . here."

"Okay. Then in you go." He urged her to the edge of the dam.

She balked. "You think the treasure is down there someplace?"

"I don't know. But if it is—this would be the place to start workin' the river," he told her. "It's easier to train the horses here than in runnin' water."

She turned and threw her arms around him. They stood together with the rain pelting them.

"If we do find it, I'll be rich, won't I?"

"You'll be the richest gal in Texas."

"And soon I'll be eighteen and I can marry anyone I want."

"If he's willing." Buchanan tried to laugh it off.

She said fiercely, "I want to marry you." She kissed him for the second time, bruising his lips. Then she was off and into the water. The blue horse followed her. In a moment they had vanished. He could hear the splashing as they swam but he could not see them. He wiped his lips. He was discomfited and confused. He did not remember having been proposed to before—at least not on a wet and dark late afternoon.

After a moment he spoke to Nightshade, rubbed the rope along his neck and over his velvet nose. Then he waded into the dam. The water was icy. He shivered for the time it took for him to become somewhat accustomed to it.

Somewhere high above the massive storm a breath of wind nudged a bank of clouds. An eerie shaft of near-light came through. Buchanan could see Blue, moving in a circle. Then the girl's head appeared as she took in a breath of needed air. She turned, saw him, smiled, nodded. The horse and Patricia Ann were already working together. He feared only the lightning now. It was a desperate chance to take, working in the storm, but he knew no other way to avoid the Farmington forces.

He took a deep breath and dove. Swimming under water, he tugged at the rope, grown promptly heavy as it grew wet. Yet he felt Nightshade move in the general direction which he had indicated.

He came up for air and found himself within a few feet of Patricia Ann. She cried, "It works! It works!"

"Great horseflesh," he told her. "Now try for the falls. See if we can get them underneath."

"What for?"

"In case we're ever trapped here. There's protection among the rocks."

"It's mighty tetchy in there." She treaded water. "I been there plenty times."

"Let's try it." He was looking for a grotto, a sub-stream rather than subterranean grotto, but he did not want to raise her hopes or cause her to be reckless in search for what was a glimmering in his mind.

They swam for the falls. The water thundered down, heavy with the addition of the flow from the mountain storm. The weird light continued, however, and they dove several times. Buchanan could see nothing, could feel nothing with outstretched, probing hands.

They came up together again. She said admiringly, "Not many people can stay under as long as me."

"It ain't somethin' I care about," he admitted, blowing out a spray. "Looks like we done all we could. Better go in before we both come down with somethin'."

"I'm beginnin' to like it," she said.

"The horses ain't."

"Yeah. Old Blue, he likes warm water."

"Nightshade don't much like it except for drinkin' purposes. He just goes along with me," said Buchanan.

They swam for shore, the horses now going ahead, anxious for land, wet or dry. There was another crack of thunder as they came ashore. The lightning slashed nearby and the girl flew into Buchanan's arms and stood, wet, shivering, plastered to him. Over her head he saw the remnants of the old fort from where he had first observed Patricia Ann bathing nude in the waters of the dam.

Something in his mind clicked as though a lantern had

been flashed on. He held her until she stopped trembling. Then he said, "Let's get back to the ranch. I want to look at the maps again."

"I'm scared again." She did not want to turn him loose. "I'm real scared."

He put her away, then lifted her into the wet saddle. "Ride hard and you'll be warmed up by the time we reach the ranch. And . . . you're not all that scared."

She laughed and slapped her heels against Blue and they were off, flying into the dwindling storm. The sun was westering and when the winds blew there was a reflected slight sunset, scarcely a wisp, beyond the mountains which led down to the brasada. They neither saw nor heard anyone, not even a small animal, all the way home.

Buchanan toweled himself vigorously, dressed slowly, thinking hard. The fort was built, he thought, some fifty years after the Cuesta expedition had been ambushed. The course of the stream had not altered, therefore the fort had full use of it. It had been a handy site for them, far better than most frontier outposts. It had been abandoned when the Comanches were decimated, he knew. But there was a connection between the fort and the stream. There had to be. The problem was to work out the importance of this fact that had been overlooked by the hundreds of searchers of the treasure.

He went down into Molly's office. Consuela brought hot coffee and tacos. Rafe stood hipshot against the door. Patricia Ann sat on the floor, her hair flowing and damp, smiling at Buchanan.

Molly said from behind the desk, "You're damn fools, both of you. Riskin' yourselves—and good horseflesh."

"Can I see the maps again?" Buchanan asked.

She went to the safe. The storm had lessened so that the rain fell in small shivers of showers.

Buchanan came off his chair. He flew across to a window, reaching for the rifle on the wall. There was a scrambling sound from without, then the clumping of hoofs as a horse fled in the mud.

"How did you know?" demanded Rafe. "I scouted around just afore comin' into the house."

"The old man would have 'em out as soon as the rain slowed down," said Buchanan.

"I believe you got a third ear," Rafe said.

"When you're up against smart folks like old Judson you have to get to thinkin' like they think," Buchanan told him.

"Like you're half crook." Molly grinned at him. "I always had a suspicion about you. Special where women are concerned."

"I'll thank you to watch your speech," Buchanan told her. He made sure the windows were tightly shuttered, then opened the old map and the newer ones. He corroborated what he had thought about the fort. He rolled up the maps and returned them to the safe.

"You learned something," Molly said.

"Not for sure. Tomorrow I'll take a little ride. Jimson and Pecos will be upstream. Someone will follow me. Maybe Rafe or Patricia Ann could spot who's doin' what by takin' to the roof."

"The roof?"

"Best lookout place," he said. "I don't want any of you in danger. Just check 'em out as best you can."

"But you'll be alone." Patricia Ann scowled. "They could backshoot you."

"They can do that anytime," Buchanan said calmly. "Wouldn't be surprised if they tried."

"You ought to have somebody along."

Buchanan said, "Maybe I got three eyes, too. Because I only been backshot a couple times in my whole life."

"It only takes once," snapped Molly.

"That'll be time enough." He looked at Consuela, who dimpled in return. "Tell me, did your grandfather ever work for the army?"

"Why, yes, Señor Buchanan." She was surprised. "How did you know?"

Buchanan twinkled at her. "If I'd known, I wouldn't have asked, now, would I? He scout against the Indians?"

"But yes. The Comanches, they always raided during the moon, you know? Into Mexico, wherever they rode. My grandfather, he hated them."

"So he was at the fort a lot?"

"Of course."

"Grotto," said Buchanan. "Words mean different things to different people."

"I do not understand," Consuela said, frowning.

"Neither do I. Not yet." Buchanan munched the last taco. "This here just makes me hungry."

"Supper will be ready." Consuela disappeared, skirts flying. Patricia Ann rose to help in the kitchen.

Buchanan said, "You stay close until I get back from the fort, you hear?"

"Like you say. Only—you oughta have somebody along."

"We talked about that." He watched her leave the room. "Molly, that's some gal you got there."

"She knows it. You know it. I ain't too sure about it," said Molly sighing. "Wild as a coot. Headstrong as a kickin' bronc."

"Molly?"

"What?"

"You mind that time in Frisco we got into the scrap at the theater?"

"Now, that was different."

"Uh-huh. You kicked that fella right where he lived. Then you dumped a bottle over the head of another one and then you pulled up your skirts and kicked a third one under the chin. Nice legs you had, too."

She said, "They were drunken bums." She stopped, stared at him. Then she yanked her skirts up to her knees. "Anything wrong with my legs now?"

Buchanan said, "I rest my case, your honor." He grinned at her. "And they're still great legs."

He offered his arm and led her to the kitchen where the odor of food was calling to him.

Brogan shook the rain from his poncho, changed his pants and boots, and went from the bunkhouse to where Judson Farmington awaited him by the open fire. Hal Farmington was drinking whiskey, his chin on his chest. The old man asked, "Well? What did you learn?"

"They're up to somethin'. They got them two jaspers buyin' minin' tools in town. The gal and Buchanan were out in the storm but I dunno where, it was too dark, too rainy to follow 'em. They were talkin' a lot." He scratched his head. "The window was closed and I couldn't hear. But that damn Buchanan, I swear he smelled me. I took off just in time."

"Mining tools? In this weather?"

"That's what the breed kid from the store told me. We can pick them up tomorrow, or whenever the weather breaks, no trouble there."

Hal said, "And split our force."

"Well, if Buchanan and the gal and the old lady and the gimpy waddy and the Mex gal go in different directions, seems like we need help—or we split up," said Brogan.

"The maps," said Judson. "Buchanan found some clue in the maps."

"Whatever the boss says, we'll do it," Brogan said. "It's a real merry-go-round and that damn Buchanan's a somethin' or other. He couldn't of seen me outside the window in the rain. How'd he know I was there?"

"You escaped, that's enough," said Judson impatiently. "I don't believe in the super powers of the bastard. He's big and tough and experienced but he certainly cannot match us in brains."

Hal stirred uneasily. Brogan simply waited, concealing whatever doubts he may have had. The old man stared into the fire. The rain beat against the sturdy house.

Finally Judson said, "Buchanan. Concentrate on him. No matter what he does, how foolish it seems. Keep an eye on him. Hal, you will act as liaison."

His son touched his swollen face.

Judson said, "Oh, you need not be seen. I wouldn't want the object of your affections to observe what Buchanan has done unto you."

Hal finished his drink, poured another.

Brogan said, "Trouble is, Buchanan always knows where ev'body is at. Like a damn Injun."

"It would seem so." Judson considered. "You are the best plainsman, eh, Brogan?"

"Symes is good."

"But Joe Glass, who is injured, is the least."

"Right now, mebbe."

"Send Glass to watch the two with the mining tools. That will keep him away from Buchanan."

"Right, Boss. He's liable to gun Buchanan anytime he sets eyes on him."

"You and Symes try to keep track of Buchanan."

Dubiously, Brogan said, "We can try."

"He seems to have the company of the girl at all times. This may be significant." Judson sneered at his son. "Too bad Hal could not charm her into joining us in a mutual search for the treasure."

Hal finished his drink.

Brogan said, "This storm'll break in an hour or so. I know Texas weather, which means I don't know nothin', come to think on it. But it shows signs of breakin'."

"Then be on the job. And Brogan?"

"Yes, Boss?"

"Consider yourself the leader. Your payment when we find the treasure will be increased." He paused. "In fact, due to Buchanan's interference, all of you will receive a share."

"Thanks, Boss." Brogan almost saluted, caught himself, then left the house.

Hal said a bit thickly, "I will retire now. Unless you have orders for me."

Judson did not look away from the flames. "I suggest you drink less—and practice with that gun of yours. You will act as liaison, keeping out of sight as far as is possible, reporting to me. We will both be present at the final showdown."

"That suits me."

"It should. And no more trying for the slut, you understand? Leave her to Buchanan until the end."

"I understand," Hal replied, choking back further words he went up to his room. He stood before the pier glass mirror and examined the damage Buchanan had done to him. Then he donned his under-shoulder gun and began practicing the fast draw. He continued until his right hand was sore from handling the weapon.

Downstairs Judson still looked at the fire. The serving woman came and silently piled another dry log upon it. He seemed not to notice her.

He had dreams of his own. No man, he reflected, is too old to dream. He thought of the earlier days and Boston. There had been caviar and lobster and champagne dinners. His wife had been frail, the ladies obliging. He was wealthy and young and healthy.

Then the disasters when he had been detected manipulating stocks and bonds during the war. Then gradual decline.

Now came the bitter memories. He had never been accepted on Beacon Hill; the Cabots and Lodges knew him not. Now those who had toadied to him were scornful.

So came the dream. He would return with all the money a man could need. He would see that his son married more money. And he would take his revenge. He knew all the tricks. Given the capital he would ruin those who had opposed him, flouted him. He would ruin them, drag down the famous names. He would rule Boston.

Then he could die happy. It was dream enough for a man of his years.

8

The early pink of the dawn promised another switch in Texas weather, a hot day. Buchanan rode the brasada. He inhaled the odors of after-rain with huge pleasure; the world seemed born anew. He was making a circle toward his destination.

When he had come to the oaks above the fort he climbed to a topmost branch and used his field glasses. It took some time before he discovered the man who was, with some difficulty, trailing him. Satisfied, he came down and climbed aboard Nightshade.

From thence on he made halfhearted attempts to disguise his tracks, knowing he would be unsuccessful. When he had come back to the river above the falls he knew Brogan or Symes, or both, were watching from a safe distance. He then sought Pecos and Jimson.

They were camped a few rods from the water. They had picks and shovels and a wheelbarrow. They watched him dismount and lead Nightshade to graze, loosening the bridle.

"Aimin' to stay awhile?" Jimson asked. "Want to pick the spot for diggin'? Maybe take a hand?"

Buchanan said, "It ain't funny. They're out there, one or two of 'em. I want this to look real."

"I ain't laughin' any," Jimson replied. "It's a long time since we did this kinda work."

Buchanan began pacing off, consulting a piece of blank paper he took from his vest pocket. He selected a piece of ground thoroughly soaked by the storm and pointed to it.

"This looks kinda soft."

Jimson and Pecos came to stare. They looked at Buchanan, at his slip of paper. They picked up tools.

Jimson said, "Playactin', that's what we're doin'. Right, Buchanan?"

"You're doin' a good job," he praised them. "Keep at it. I'm stayin' awhile to give 'em the idea we're onto it. That ought to bring the Farmingtons."

"You want the Farmingtons here?"

"Sooner or later that old man will be on the scene," Buchanan told them. "I'm ridin' up to the fort in about an hour. Give me that shovel."

They worked, industriously but not feverishly. They stopped at intervals to drink from canteens, to speak with one another, maintaining a cheery, expectant attitude, as if they knew exactly what they were doing.

Buchanan worked up a sweat, loosening his muscles, causing a couple of old wounds to make themselves known. Then he said, "You two know enough to keep watch. They won't take pot shots, they'll be satisfied for you to do the hard work."

"We know enough."

"Sound carries good over water. If I hear shots I'll be right on the job," he promised them.

"Course we'd prob'ly be stiffs by then," Jimson said, "but thanks, anyway."

"If you're dead, it's your own fault," Buchanan said. "Just be ready for anything."

He slipped the bridle back into the mouth of Nightshade and mounted. He rode up to the fort from which he had first observed the scene. It was a complete ruin excepting for one section.

Again he examined the terrain through the glasses. He could not detect any sign of the Farmington crew. He went to the fallen wall nearest the busy, swollen stream below. He examined it closely, allowing in his mind for the years since the fort had been abandoned.

One huge boulder lay hard against the broken wall. He reached down and tugged. It did not budge. He removed his vest and gunbelt. He bent his knees and found a hand grip. He exerted all his strength.

The boulder rolled over once. Buchanan stretched his aching back. He was looking down a tunnel.

"Uh-huh," he said aloud. "That was a culvert, all right. Waste downstream. Get fresh water upstream, tote it to the fort. No pump in them days. But the dam, now, what about the dam?"

It had to be theory now. If the treasure had been dumped into the river it would have been exposed long ago. Therefore . . . it was necessary to return to his hunch.

Once again he checked the horizon. There was one man watching him. He thought it was Symes. He put on vest and gunbelt and got aboard Nightshade. He rode back down through the brasada. He heard the rustle of cattle and flushed a trio of C-R steers that had escaped the desultory roundup of the inept cowboys. He rousted them, chased them through the tangle of thorns and wet, jutting branches. He drove them to the camp where the three boys, whom he knew to be Dobey, Buster Coy and Slater, pretended they were holding the small herd.

He said, "Cool 'em down and hold them. You got the brandin' all done?"

"What little there was of it."

"Then stay here and do your job as best you can." They were too green, too young to be of any further use. "I'll be out to check on you later."

"Okay, Boss."

He rode back, sweating now, covered with brambles and with every excuse to take a cooling swim. He settled Nightshade down to a pace which would not lather him. He was being followed, he knew, but at a distance which did not disturb him too much.

When he arrived at the edge of the dam Patricia Ann was already swimming slowly around with the rope attached to the saddle of Blue. On the shore was the contraption manufactured by Rafe. He shucked his outer clothing and attached Rafe's invention to the saddle and led the big black horse into the cooling water of the overfull dam.

Patricia shouted, "Real nice day for it, huh, Tom?"

Unnecessarily loud, knowing voices carry over water, he boomed, "Ran three of your cows in. Got mighty hot."

He remained on the near side of Nightshade, allowing him to drink, arranging the reins so that they could not trail. He slid out of his clothing, so that he wore only the cutoff Levi's. The Farmington spy could only be on the far side, among the trees. The idea was to make it seem that Buchanan was going in for a pleasurable cooling off after his ride. He rolled up his shirt, torn by the thorns of the brasada, and placed it alongside his pants, boots and socks. He deposited his hat atop the pile. He spoke into the ear of Nightshade, bidding him stay. Then he dove into the rain-deepened dam.

He swam out to where Patricia Ann and the blue horse were frolicking. He turned on his back and floated. They came together and he spoke in lowered voice.

"Consuela's grandma knew something. Maybe they didn't want the treasure discovered until it suited 'em. Anyway, the army built a culvert. And I believe, what they did, they covered the grotto."

"You mean it's in there somewhere near here?"

"That's the notion. I ain't sure."

"But that's pretty deep down."

"You said you're the best swimmer in Texas."

"I said it and I mean it."

"I ain't. But you and me, we're goin' to play like we're challengin' each other. To stay under water."

"You know where the place is?"

"No. We got to find it. May not be able to do it right quick. But it's worth the tryin'. They're watchin' us," he warned. "They got Jimson and Pecos under their eye, too. And maybe somebody watchin' the house. I don't believe they'll start shootin'. Anyway, we'll start beneath the falls. Seems like that would be a natural place."

"We keep the horses nearby?"

"Make it look like play," he warned her. "And in case they do start shootin' keep the horses under the falls and behind the rocks."

"If they shoot Blue . . . or Nightshade . . ."

"Don't think about it."

She nodded, her face cloudy. They swam in leisurely fashion. The falls were heavy due to the rain. They dove beneath them. Buchanan came up first, blowing, and gave a low whistle. Nightshade walked into the water and swam toward him. Buchanan unfastened one end of the rope with which to guide him. He dove with it in his hand. Nightshade did not like it much beneath the falls but his long training with his owner kept him staunch.

He was beginning to worry about Patricia Ann, who had been underwater for so long when her head popped up near him. She blew out water for a moment, then spoke in his ear.

"I found a hole. Like a cave."

"Grotto," said Buchanan.

"But there are rocks piled all around it, blockin' it."

"Came downriver," Buchanan said. "It figures."

"But how can we move the rocks?"

"Have to look," said Buchanan. "You stay and hold the horses. Watch over by the trees when you can."

"I'll tug your rope if anything happens."

"Uh-huh." Buchanan took a huge breath and swam down into the clear, cold water. When he could see in the depths he at once perceived the rocks covering what appeared to be the mouth of a cavern. It was close to where the army culvert had been dug. He made a slip knot of the rope attached to Nightshade and began to explore. The rocks were large and his weightlessness was a problem. He managed to roll away a few of the smaller ones. There was undoubtedly a cave.

He could no longer hold his breath. He swam upward with haste. The girl was floating near the horses.

He said, "You found somethin'."

"Is it . . . is it the grotto?"

"It'll take a lot of divin' and a lot of work to find out." He rested, hand on Nightshade's flank.

"What if it *is* there?"

"We'll get the gear we need to bring it out."

"Then the Farmingtons'll know what we're up to."

"Then the Farmingtons'll take their best shot," he promised her. "Nobody said it would be easy."

"I'll go down again. I can stay under longer than you."

He agreed. "Move the smaller rocks. We got to get inside the place."

"The grotto," she murmured, taking her deep inhalation.

She went under. He watched the obvious place of concealment for a spy. He thought he detected movement in the copse of trees. He put a hand on the bundle which Rafe had contrived, waiting. Nothing happened. All was still again.

Mrs. Bascomb fed chicken soup to Rusty Wallace. He was sitting up in the bed, uneasy as a badger. "The town is very quiet."

- "Then there's mischief afoot," he growled. "They all crawl into their holes for fear of shootin' trouble."

She hesitated, then said, "When I was at the store I think I discovered something."

"What?"

"Well, you know that half-breed boy, Pancho?"

"He works in the store."

"But he's been taking off at odd times. Runs away, then comes back. I think he's spying for the Farmingtons since McGee's is closed."

"And he's been talkin' amongst his own folks. Which is why they're layin' low."

"I don't know about that. I only know that it is peaceful and you must rest."

"Rest? I've rested my fool head off. I tell you, somethin' is up."

"You can't do anything about it right now," she said. "There . . . eat the good soup."

"Buchanan. If I could only hear from Buchanan."

"As soon as you're well enough we'll hire a buggy," she promised. "We'll drive out to the C-R and visit."

"A buggy!" He scowled. "Me in a damn buggy driven by a woman."

"I'm sorry, Rusty."

He softened. "I don't know what would've become of me before now if it wasn't for you, woman," he said softly.

She flushed. "Thank you, Rusty."

She wiped the soup from his lips and went into the kitchen with the bowl and platter. She stood by the sink and pressed her hands to her eyes. He was the kindest, best man she had ever met and she feared in her heart that she would lose him.

Hal Farmington tied up at the rack and went into the house. His father was in the office poring over old maps. The whiskey decanter was in evidence and the son poured himself a drink. He was sullen.

His father demanded, "Well? Give me a report."

"Jimson and Pecos are digging near the edge of the stream, above the dam. I watched. They were not working too hard. Their hearts are not in it."

"The house?"

"Señora Cuesta, the Mex girl and the lame man are moving about, busy at one thing and another. Nothing cogent that I could ascertain."

"Buchanan. Where is Buchanan?"

"He and the girl are bathing. As though on a picnic. Much fun and laughter and all that."

His father grunted. "Irks you, does it?"

"Certainly not."

"Ha! They are in the dam?"

"Beneath the waterfalls, mainly. Their horses seem to enjoy it as much as they do."

"Brogan is watching them?"

"He is."

"Smart, that Brogan. Possibly too smart. On the other hand . . ." He traced a bent finger across the map. "The dam. Water. Everyone who has a soupçon of imagination is aware that the Cuesta expedition did not have time to bury the treasure. Now, there is the fort. Built fifty years after the expedition."

"Abandoned, crumbling. It has been dug over and over by searchers."

"We know that. But the water. Under the water. If I knew, if we could properly read that old map . . . "

"Yes, sir?"

"Buchanan has it. No doubt about it. Pancho believes he saw it given him by that fool woman, Mrs. Bascomb."

"Where is Pancho?"

"At hand. I may need him." Judson scratched his chin. He looked again at the map, asked idly, "You say Buchanan and the slut were swimming beneath the falls?"

"Well, diving a lot. As if they were vying with each other to see who could stay under the longest."

The old man stared. "Diving?"

"Yes. Taking turns."

Judson slapped his hand down so hard the map jumped from the desk and floated to the floor. "God! Not only must I fight this damned Buchanan but I have fools all about me! I have a fool for a son who sees only the bulges of a slutty half-breed girl and not an inch beyond!"

"I . . . I don't know what you mean." He recognized

the oncoming wild rage. He swallowed hard. "They're just—swimming on a hot day."

"Diving! Staying under water. Oh, you utter fool! Jimson and the other dividing our forces. Everyone practicing thin deceits to throw me off! It's as plain as the day. Call in the nigger. Get Symes and Brogan together at the dam. I will attend to the rest."

"But the law . . . We can't just attack them, for no reason."

"There is no law. Wallace is dying in town. The nearest federal marshal is a hundred miles away. I want all our valuables packed, you understand? The wagons that I provided for that purpose. I want to be ready to leave. . . . But first I want the equipment to go beneath water, the block and falls, everything with which to hoist heavy objects, men, everything. Do you understand, you dolt?"

"But . . . but Father . . . "

"Buchanan! He's the key. He knows the country. He has discovered the treasure. You think I will allow that thundering bully, that widow and slut, to beat me to the treasure? To prevent our return to civilization in triumph? Thank God I have the brains, at least, to avoid such defeat. Now, go, damn it, go and do what I say!"

Hal fled, happy to get out of the storm. The old man waited until he heard the sound of departing hoofbeats. Then he said, "Pancho."

The boy came from the next room where he had been listening. Judson produced a gold coin.

"You have had silver. Now it is gold," said the elder Farmington. "You will go to the C-R ranch. You will tell the people there that Buchanan needs them. At the dam. You understand."

The boy nodded, never taking his eyes from the coin that represented wealth to him.

"You will wait a certain time. Enough time, you know?"

"*Sí*, señor."

"Then, when all are gone, you will set fire to the house in the manner which I have described. The coal oil. You knw where it is?"

"*Sí*, señor."

"The house, the stable, everything. I want nothing left standing. I want complete destruction."

The boy did not understand the words, but he recognized the emotion. "*Sí*, señor. As you say."

"There will be more gold."

The dark eyes gleamed. "*Sí*, señor. *Gracias*."

"Go, then." He proffered the coin, the boy seized it, and skittered from the room.

Judson Farmington sat back. It was time to see to the rifle, to saddle up. Once the treasure was located he would have it in his hands so quickly that no one would ever quite know what happened. He knew where he was going to convey it to a railway junction. He had already forged the papers he might need, a conveyance of ownership, identification of himself and Hal under assumed names. He had planned for a long time. Now, if the living legend, Buchanan, had arrived at the same conclusions that he, Judson Farmington, had deducted—he was once more a wealthy man. His return to Boston would be a victory pageant, he promised himself.

Buchanan was down for the tenth time. They had removed enough of the round stones, worn by the water of a hundred years, so that they could make out dimly a cavern of good size. He reached for the last big block which barred entrance to the water-filled cave.

It came loose. But it was a keystone and two larger

hunks of rock slid into Buchanan's left arm. He was pinned, he could not extricate himself. And he had expanded the air in his lungs by too far.

He tugged at the rope. On the surface Nightshade swam, his teeth bared, kicking, tail elevated. Patricia Ann watched. Puzzled, then alarmed. She dove.

She floated into Buchanan. She tugged at the rock. He was choking on water, now. Nightshade swam above. Buchanan made a mighty last effort.

The rocks budged as Patricia Ann assailed them, furious that she had little strength underwater. The rope tightened. Buchanan's arm scraped, then came free, bruised. He had barely enough strength to aid him in his progress to the surface.

He drew into his tortured lungs. He looked at his arm, which was beginning to swell. Patricia Ann came popping up beside him.

She cried, "Are you hurt bad, Tom?"

"Not that bad." But the arm was not at full strength, he realized. Purple and red began to show beneath the skin.

She said, "We can get in, now. That last bunch of rocks, they opened a big hole."

"Doggone near opened me." He rubbed his arm as best he could. The cold water numbed the pain.

"I got to go down and see if we're onto it," she said.

"Yes." He needed to rest his lungs. "You do that. I'll watch."

Buchanan caught a flicker of movement in the trees again. It was not as surreptitious as it had been. He swam nearer to the contraption that Rafe had invented.

Patricia Ann came up after what seemed an age. He knew the moment he saw her bright eyes. She raised a hand and something glittered in the sunlight.

He said, "No! Keep it under water."

It was, he knew, too late. She had been unable to refrain from showing him a gold trinket. Gold, he knew, resisted the tarnish of water, the only metal that would retain its gleaming color.

He said, "Back! Under the falls."

It was at that moment he heard the sound of a buckboard on the other side of the dam. He craned and saw Molly, Consuela and Rafe getting down, coming toward the water, heard Molly call, "Tom! What is it? What's wrong?"

He shouted, "Get down! Take cover!"

The first shots rang out from the copse of trees across the way. One of the horses drawing the buckboard screamed and went down.

"Shoot the other horse! Take cover!" Buchanan yelled. He was reaching inside the bundle on Nightshade.

Rafe moved with dispatch. He put a pistol to the head of the second horse. He dragged Molly and Consuela behind out of sight, then went to work to add the buckboard to the barrier.

Patricia Ann said, "They know we found it! I gave it away!"

"Get your gun and stay put," Buchanan ordered her. "Don't waste any time cryin' over spilt gold!"

He saw a movement in the trees and fired. He heard a yell. Someone had been pinked, he knew. It would surprise them, they had no way of knowing that he was armed, there in the water beneath the falls.

But he had never underestimated old Farmington. There was only a certain length of time that Patricia Ann and he could remain in the cold water. They were already chilled. They would suffer from exposure with the coming of night.

He rested his left arm on Nightshade's neck. He had to hold the rifle in such a way that it could not be impeded by dampness. Patricia Ann was making a fair job of it, but it was too much to ask of the girl.

Jimson and Pecos were upstream. If they heard shooting and rushed down pell-mell they were on the wrong side of the stream. They could be cut down before they realized what was going on, Buchanan thought, worrying.

He heard old Farmington's high voice calling, "Spread out. Hold your fire. Glass, you can have Buchanan now. Any way to take care of him. The treasure's down there someplace and by God, it's ours."

Patricia Ann was maneuvering the horses to the protection of outcropping rock. The gold trinket was stuffed into her bodice of bandanna handkerchiefs. And a lot of good it would do her, Buchanan lamented, if he couldn't figure a way out of this, fighting against pure hatred and greed—and paid, practiced gunmen—and the water, which was becoming colder and colder. The numbness was wearing off and his left arm hurt. He wondered if a bone was broken.

He said to the girl, "Steady yourself across the saddle."

Shots began skipping into the falls. They were uncomfortably close. Sooner or later, he thought, they would be caught either by direct hit or a ricochet.

The people from the ranch were tied down. They dared not expose themselves to the marksman across the dam. Buchanan poked out his rifle, waited for the flash of a gun from the woods, then began firing.

He laid shots in a line, crisscrossing back. Patricia Ann followed suit. There was a scrambling retreat in the trees and someone was heard yelling, "What's he got in there, a Gatlin' gun or somethin'?"

Farmington yelled, "We must get them! All of them!"

No one responded. The shots were wilder now. The fire laid down by Patricia Ann and Buchanan had driven them back. They were, after all, gunslingers, not soldiers, Buchanan reflected. He looked at the girl. She had defiantly placed the golden object around her throat. It was a necklace with a pendant which he could not distinguish.

She said, "You know what, Tom?"

"Not right now, I don't know anything."

"Well, I know I hate prunes. And we're both beginnin' to look like 'em."

"At least we're live prunes, up 'til now."

She said, "You think we'll get out of this?"

"I always think there's a chance."

"Fightin' from here, in water?"

"There's always a way," he told her, not having the slightest notion what way it could be now, with the two of them in this predicament. "Be right careful."

"I'm already reloaded," she said proudly.

"Good girl." He filled the magazine of the Remington. He replaced it under the waterproof. "I'm goin' down and take a look. If anything moves, shoot it."

He dove. His arm ached and the opening into the grotto was a tight fit. He blinked until he could see the treasure.

It lay in some confusion but it was all there. He could detect gold ingots, encrusted silver plate, jewels covered with fungus. It was a fortune, all right, he thought. It had brought vast disappointment to hard labors; it had brought death. But it was all there, the Cuesta treasure. It only remained for him to save it for the rightful heirs. He made his way painfully back to the surface of the dam. The waterfall was diminishing in force, the rains spent. There was no sign of action from the enemy.

Molly's voice called over the water. "Patricia Ann?"

"We're all right, Ma."

Buchanan said, "Keep your heads down!"

Rafe answered, "We got guns enough, Buchanan. We can hold 'em."

"You do that." It started a train of thought. He asked the girl, "Can you handle two rifles and keep 'em dry and ready?"

"I . . . I don't know."

He said, "We can't last here. All they have to do is wait us out."

"Couldn't we get to Ma and Rafe in the dark?"

"They'll be goin' around that way," Buchanan said. "They can hit them from the rear, don't you see?"

"Oh, no!"

"I can swim under water. But I can't carry regular guns and keep 'em dry." He rummaged in his saddlebag and brought out a Bowie knife that he had not handled in years. He found his belt containing the little derringer with two extra .45 charges. He managed to gird himself with it, knowing the buckle was especially designed to be waterproof.

She said, "You ain't goin' after that crew with those weapons, Tom. They'll kill you for sure."

"Nothin's for sure in this world," he told her.

"Tom, I can't let you do that!"

"I'll drift downstream. If Jimson and Pecos show, maybe it'll create some fuss," he went on, disregarding her protest. "Remember, with Rusty laid up there's no law hereabouts. They could kill us all and get away."

"No, it's not right. Maybe we can dicker with 'em."

"No way to trust 'em."

"But Tom . . ."

He pointed with his right arm. "Look yonder."

There was a faint glow in the sky. It was in the direction of the C-R ranch house. She cried out.

He said, "They're burnin' the house. You see what that means? They got to get all of us."

"I'm the best swimmer," she said. "I've got to go with you."

"You got to stay here and keep firin' if they move."

"Tom, please."

"Only way I see it," he said. "You stand tight."

She threw a wet arm around him and gave him a watery kiss on the mouth. "Tom, I can't let you go."

"Girl, you can't stop me." He took the deepest breath he had yet managed. Then he slipped under water and into the current of the still swollen, fast-moving stream.

The weight of the belt and the heavy Bowie helped, but it was a strain to stay beneath the surface for as long as he thought he should. When his lungs were near bursting, he swam to the shore and cautiously popped his head above, into the clear, fresh air. He was in time to hear shots.

He oriented himself. The Farmington bunch were now shooting at the buckboard and the dead horse barricade. The return fire came promptly from Patricia Ann. She was handling both rifles with skill. Buchanan felt he could go forward boldly. He swam into the stream and again went beneath the surface.

He drifted with the current. He swam. He came up for air. His left arm throbbed. Now he had to make it across the stream, he knew. He listened, heard voices upstream. He rested a moment, then realized he was stiffening up from the exposure and his injury. He dove toward the far shore and put every ounce of his remaining energy to task.

When he finally came ashore at the far end of the

stand of oaks, he lay very still for several moments, expanding and contracting his muscles, regaining breath.

He was almost naked, bootless, with a long blade and a tiny gun as his only weapons. One arm was practically useless by now. There were the two Farmingtons, Brogan, Symes and the black man who wanted worst of them all to kill him.

He moved into the trees. Without his boots the going was painful in the extreme. Still, he moved with all the stealth and skill he had acquired in his many years on the frontier. He made no sound; he sought cover at every opportunity.

Finally he could distinguish the voice of Judson Farmington, giving orders as always. He crouched behind a huge bush, listening.

"We must surround them. Symes, can you swim?"

"Not too good."

"Someone's got to cross that stream and get behind those people behind the wagon. Two women and a cripple. They should be easiest to be rid of. Remember, all must go. You saw the house burning. It is all or nothing now. The retreat we shall make is complete, we have nothing to fear."

Brogan said, "I can swim good."

"I'd rather have you here, with me."

The old man was careful, Buchanan thought. Brogan was the smartest and the most dangerous. Excepting, he added to himself, possibly the black man.

At that moment Joe Glass, separated from the rest, his arm still in a sling, came straight past the bush where Buchanan was hidden.

There was a moment of indecision, then Buchanan made his move. He stole close to the moving figure, snapped his right arm around his throat. Glass was a powerful man. He thrashed and kicked.

Buchanan put the knife to his chest. He whispered, "You want to die right here? Or you want to give up?"

Glass stopped struggling, his eyes fixed on the gleaming Bowie. Buchanan rapped him alongside the head with his fist. The black man dropped like a poled ox.

Buchanan used the neckerchief, the man's belt and a piece of trailing, wet vine. He gagged Glass and tied him up in a fashion he had learned from the Indians of the plains in years gone by. He said, "If you do get loose, it'll be too late. So think hard."

He examined the rifle and the revolver of the man who lay trussed, staring at him with pure hatred. He thrust the Bowie into his belt. He clutched the rifle in his good hand and held the short gun loosely in the aching left hand.

He crept toward the voices he could now plainly hear. There was scant brush behind which to conceal himself, but they were far from expecting an attack from this direction. Symes was covering northward, the direction from which Jimson and Pecos had not appeared. Buchanan wondered if they had turned tail, feeling the battle lost. If there was one thing he needed now it was a diversion of some sort.

There was the sound of a horse running. The Mexican boy, Pancho, rode in on Molly's favorite white. He had taken the trouble to steal a silver-spangled show saddle, which he strode with something less than natural grace. He was very proud of himself. He carried a rifle. He dismounted and saluted Farmington.

"It is done," he proclaimed. "The *rancho* is destroy."

Buchanan whispered to himself, "You're mighty young to die, there, boy. Mighty young."

Farmington was saying, "So far, so good. We can

wait out Buchanan and the girl. Then we can deal with those across the river."

The boy was bursting with importance. He waved an arm. "The marshal. He comes soon."

"Marshal Wallace? He's dyin' in bed!" said Brogan.

Before Bunchanan could act there was the rattle of harness and the sound of wheels. A wagon barreled toward them, a team of grays heaving and lathered. Mrs. Bascomb, pale and drawn, bonnet blown off back and hanging by its strings, was driving. Wallace sat propped beside her, a shotgun in his hands. Deathily pale, he was scarcely able to remain erect. Still, he managed to speak.

"You're all under arrest by the authority granted me as marshal of Yaqui."

Every weapon turned upon the marshal and the woman. Buchanan gathered himself.

Farmington screeched, "You old fool! You should have stayed to die in your bed with your female beside you!"

Wallace said, "If I die, a few of you go with me. This here is loaded with buck." He held the shotgun over his knees, pointed at them. "Don't anybody move."

Buchanan started from his hiding place. The Mexican boy, unnoticed, picked up a stone. He threw it.

The stone hit the horse attached to the buggy. The reaction was immediate. As the horse leaped, Wallace was thrown off balance. The shotgun exploded harmlessly into the branches of the trees. Brogan and Symes were in action at once. They seized the gun, dragged both occupants from the buggy, roughed them to earth.

Buchanan, in the open, was committed. It was against his grain, against his entire being, to shoot down people indiscriminately. He knew they deserved no better. It would be easy enough, even with one hand, to reduce them so that they could not fight him further. Yet he spoke, his voice harsh and commanding.

"That does it. Drop your guns."

They whirled, staring. For a moment he thought he had them. Brogan and Symes, gunwise, knew the danger. The sight of him, almost naked, hugh, imposing, was enough to stop any sane person.

But Judson Farmington screamed, "Kill him!"

Buchanan watched the old man come around with light rifle. He could not hesitate. He fired from the hip.

Farmington spun, still howling. The slight diversion gave Brogan enough time to make a lightning draw of his revolver.

Buchanan shot him with the gun in his damaged left hand. Symes dropped to one knee, showing his experience, and got off a shot. It hit Buchanan in the left shoulder. It threw him off balance. The boy was aiming the rifle.

From out of the water came Patricia Ann. She held a rifle dripping wet. She swung it with all her might. She clubbed the boy on his right ear. He fell and rolled, wordless, unconscious.

Buchanan recovered. He stepped to one side as Symes fired again. Unable to lever the rifle, he dropped it. He flipped the revolver he had taken from Glass into his right hand. He shot Symes between the eyes.

Hal Farmington had not moved. He seemed stunned by the sudden bloodbath. Patricia Ann crouched, staring at him, then at Buchanan.

Young Farmington did not have a weapon in his hands. Buchanan motioned to him. "Just stay like you are."

The young man's eyes flickered. His father now lay quite still. Symes was dead. Brogan groaned, his life leaking away. The boy was inert, yards away. Mrs. Bascomb was struggling to get to the prone marshal.

The dream was dying in Hal Farmington. He started to make his draw, then stopped. He looked helplessly at Buchanan, then at the girl. He spoke in a queer, uneven voice.

"I . . . do not . . . like . . . killing."

Patricia Ann stepped briskly to him and removed the gun from beneath his shoulder. She said, "And a good thing, too, since you're still alive."

"I . . . my father . . . " Then he shut his lips firmly. "I've been wrong. I surrender."

Patricia Ann said cheerfully, "You already been beat to pieces. So just do like Tom says."

Buchanan began examination of the damage. Brogan tried to grin at him.

"I told the old bastard. I said you was a livin' legend. , . . Like they put in them books. . . . I told him. . . ."

Brogan died.

The boy could not be more than sixteen, Buchanan thought. His neck was twisted. There was no pulse. Patricia Ann had broken him.

Judson lay nearby. The old man had very little life left but he had the strength to speak, glaring at Buchanan.

"You bloody fool. You ruined everything."

"Does that make me a fool?"

"And you . . . " He spat blood toward his son. "That I ever whelped you! You miserable, puling coward!"

"But he's got more sense than you have," Buchanan observed. "I think you're goin' over, Farmington. You got anything decent to say?"

"May you and this miserable hell of a country be wiped from the earth. May you all burn in hell."

"Father!" Hal's voice was anguished. "Please, don't carry hatred into the grave."

"Damn you all!" croaked the old man.

In all his life Buchanan had been moved to see men, good and bad, die of violence or disease. Now he stood and watched and was unconcerned. It was like watching the death of a maddened animal.

Hal said, "He was demented. Truly, he was."

"Uh-huh," said Buchanan. "He was crazy, all right."

Jimson's voice sounded from the woods. "You all okay in there?"

Buchanan said dryly, "Uh-huh. Thanks for the help."

"We had trouble gettin' down. And then at the end, there, we was scared of hittin' you or the gal."

It was pointless to argue. Buchanan's shoulder was now giving him serious pain. He said, "You're in time to clean up the mess. Bury 'em, or whatever Wallace wants. Later you can get some gear, block and falls, whatever we need to work under water."

"You found it? The Cuesta treasure?"

Buchanan said, "Just obey orders, Jimson. Understand?"

He would never know whether they had ducked the fight in hopes of somehow getting the treasure for themselves, or if Jimson was telling the truth. It didn't matter. They were rolling their eyes at the dead bodies. They were no better nor any worse than hundreds he had encountered. They would be needed to help with the work ahead.

He went to where Mrs. Bascomb held Rusty's head in her lap. He said, "Rusty, you damn fool, you somehow managed to save it. Close, but it worked."

"The law . . . I always been . . . I'm the only law hereabouts."

"You'll get a share. It's a mighty big haul, the Cuesta treasure."

"Not me, I won't get anything. But the kids . . . " Wallace coughed.

Buchanan picked him up and put him in the buggy. He needed only one arm to handle the frail body. He said, "Mrs. Bascomb, get him to the doctor. And tell Gonzales I'll be in to see him soon as I can get there."

"Oh, is someone else hurt?" she asked.

"Only me." He was bleeding now. He managed to signal across the river to Molly and Consuela and Rafe. He was really worn down to a nubbin, he thought. He never remembered being so weary, so drained. He looked at Patricia Ann. "We'll have to hitch Nightshade and Blue and take everybody to the ranch. This one, too," he gestured toward Hal.

Patricia Ann said, "You forgettin', Tom? There probably ain't a ranch anymore."

"Oh, Lord. I'd forgotten. Reckon my head ain't workin' too god. Jimson!"

The man came quickly.

"You and Pecos get across the river. Bring that wagon over here."

"But . . . but how . . . ?"

"Do it," Buchanan said. He sat down on a fallen tree. "Just do it. Patricia Ann, you help him."

The marshal's buggy was rolling toward town. The girl looked rebellious for a moment. Then she went back into the water, the gold necklace gleaming. Buchanan looked at young Farmington.

"All that trouble. All these dead folks. You think that treasure can make up for it?"

Farmington did not answer. The spirit had gone out of him, the dream was ended.

9

The jeweler had come over from El Paso by stage. He was known to Buchanan, who trusted him. His name was Eli Jackson. They gathered in the house in town that they had been forced to rent. Building was even then going on as imported workmen essayed to reconstruct the C-R ranch as it had once stood, bright and staunch against the Texas northers and the Texas sun.

"A hundred thousand in gold," said Jackson. "But you knew that."

Buchanan adjusted the sling in which he was carrying his left arm. "Gold is one thing. Jewels is another."

Jackson, a wry man in black alpaca, said, "I can't be definite. But when they are all cleaned up I should judge their worth at close to a quarter million. They are very ancient. Many are museum pieces."

"I ain't sellin' the prettiest ones," Molly said. "They're

for me and Patricia Ann. Exceptin' what Tom wants. Tom?"

He said, "That thing Patricia Ann wore in the water."

"That is pure gold with a ruby pendant," Jackson told him.

"There's a little lady married to a boy named Billy Buttons over in New Mexico," Buchanan said. "It'll look right pretty on her. If there's a tiny bracelet or somethin' not too important. Their baby might like to gnaw on it."

"We owe you money," said she.

"Okay," said Buchanan wearily. "But Rusty Wallace, he deserves a heap—whatever you say. Jimson and Pecos will earn their thousand before they're finished. There'll be a bill to make you blink on the new house. You got to get good stock to make a decent herd for next year. Unless you're not countin' on ranchin'."

Molly said firmly, "I'm a ranch woman. Patricia Ann is a ranch gal."

He looked at Patricia Ann. His arm hurt in the sling. The girl was poring over a fashion magazine. She was wearing a store-bought dress, the best the people in El Paso could manage through the good offices of Eli Jackson. She looked different. She had not thrown herself at Buchanan lately; she was now thinking about other things. Molly would have trouble with her at that, he thought, more than he could have believed a week or so ago. But then, he had never pretended to understand women.

"That black man in the jail," said Molly. "He's telling everybody that he's going to kill you. This has been nothing but bad trouble for you, Tom."

"You can't say that's true," Buchanan told her. "I got to go see Rusty, now."

"I'll figure out what I owe you." She looked defeated, harassed. "But I never can, can I?"

"You can forget it," he said. He left and Patricia Ann seemed not to notice his going.

Rusty was sitting up in bed, Mrs. Bascomb at his side. He reached out a thin hand and said, "I'm still hangin' in there, Tom."

"Molly will take care of all expenses. You'll be able to buy two farms for your daughter if you want."

"The high country?" begged Mrs. Bascomb.

Rusty shook his head. "No way for me."

"You're goin'," Buchanan told him. "By stage, by carriage, however. My young friends in New Mexico already know. And if you're real smart you'll take this lady along."

"Why, Mr. Buchanan!" She was blushing.

"That is, if Rusty's willin' to have me send the preacher over. There is a preacher, ain't there?"

"Mr. Buchanan!"

Rusty Wallace was not looking at Buchanan. He was reaching a hand to the woman. Buchanan walked out. Nobody seemed to notice when he left a room that day.

There was an aged Mexican attending the jail. He admitted Buchanan without ceremony. Hal Farmington lay on a pallet inside a cell. Buchanan waited while the jailer opened the door. The young man sat up, haggard, pallid.

"You don't look too good," Buchanan told him.

"I won't ever feel good, either." He shook himself. "I'm not going to cry, Buchanan."

"No. You ain't all that bad," said Buchanan. "You couldn't stand up to your father. That's a shame, but it ain't a crime."

He stiffened his spine. "I'll pay for my crimes."

"Don't be a hero, son," Buchanan said dryly. "The Cuestas ain't chargin' you."

"What? I don't believe it."

"Did you order their house burned down?"

"Why . . . no. But conspiracy . . . "

"Out here that's hard to prove. You can sell your ranch, Farmington. You got a lot of years ahead. You can get the hell out of here and start somewhere else if you got the sand."

"You can't mean that!"

Buchanan extracted an official paper from his pocket. "You're loose. I wouldn't linger, though. Texas folks are mighty peculiar. I'd take the next stage out."

"You mean . . . I'm free? Right now?"

"Free as you'll ever be. I don't know how free that is."

He handed the paper to Farmington. He saw that the young man was rendered speechless. He walked to the next cell, peered in. The black man glared back at him.

"Your real name's Clarence Jameson?"

"Damn you to hell, Buchanan," said Glass.

"Funny thing, my best friend's a black man," mused Buchanan. "Now here I got one that wants to kill me."

"I'll do it. I get outa here I'll be on your trail."

Buchanan said, "If I was you, I'd think a long while before I started. Just think about it. You catch me and kill me, what does it get you?"

"It don't matter none. I'll be after you."

"There's been plenty before you," Buchanan told him. "Can't wish you luck. So long, Clarence."

He went down to the livery stable where Nightshade was growing restless by the day. He gave the boy a dollar and said, "Have him ready in an hour. I'll be leavin'."

People walked the streets of Yaqui now. The saloon had reopened under new management; Hanson waved from the general store. Buchanan paused on the steps of the house rented for the Cuestas. He took a deep breath.

He would accept the repayment of the money he had advanced. He would tell them good-bye.

He wondered if they would note that he was departing. The whole business of the Cuesta treasure seemed blurred. Certainly his relationship with Patricia Ann had evaporated. It was like a heap of other things he had encountered. He did not know whether to be glad or sorry. He mounted the steps to make his farewells.

He would soon be in the high country with his friends. He would rest, hunt, fish, lie under the stars at night. He would hear from his black friend Coco, maybe they would meet again soon. The world of Buchanan had not changed.

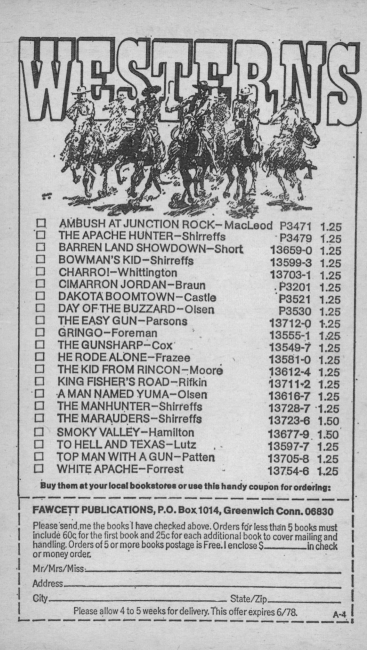

WESTERNS

☐	AMBUSH AT JUNCTION ROCK—MacLeod	P3471	1.25
☐	THE APACHE HUNTER—Shirreffs	P3479	1.25
☐	BARREN LAND SHOWDOWN—Short	13659-0	1.25
☐	BOWMAN'S KID—Shirreffs	13599-3	1.25
☐	CHARRO!—Whittington	13703-1	1.25
☐	CIMARRON JORDAN—Braun	P3201	1.25
☐	DAKOTA BOOMTOWN—Castle	P3521	1.25
☐	DAY OF THE BUZZARD—Olsen	P3530	1.25
☐	THE EASY GUN—Parsons	13712-0	1.25
☐	GRINGO—Foreman	13555-1	1.25
☐	THE GUNSHARP—Cox	13549-7	1.25
☐	HE RODE ALONE—Frazee	13581-0	1.25
☐	THE KID FROM RINCON—Moore	13612-4	1.25
☐	KING FISHER'S ROAD—Rifkin	13711-2	1.25
☐	A MAN NAMED YUMA—Olsen	13616-7	1.25
☐	THE MANHUNTER—Shirreffs	13728-7	1.25
☐	THE MARAUDERS—Shirreffs	13723-6	1.50
☐	SMOKY VALLEY—Hamilton	13677-9	1.50
☐	TO HELL AND TEXAS—Lutz	13597-7	1.25
☐	TOP MAN WITH A GUN—Patten	13705-8	1.25
☐	WHITE APACHE—Forrest	13754-6	1.25

Buy them at your local bookstore or use this handy coupon for ordering:

Louis L'Amour

THE NUMBER ONE SELLING WESTERN AUTHOR OF ALL TIME. Mr. L'Amour's books have been made into over 25 films including the giant bestseller HONDO. Here is your chance to order any or all direct by mail.

☐	CROSSFIRE TRAIL	P3495	1.25
☐	HELLER WITH A GUN	P3492	1.25
☐	HONDO	P3502	1.25
☐	KILKENNY	P3453	1.25
☐	LAST STAND AT PAPAGO WELLS	P3475	1.25
☐	SHOWDOWN AT YELLOW BUTTE	P3476	1.25
☐	THE TALL STRANGER	P3461	1.25
☐	TO TAME A LAND	P3494	1.25
☐	UTAH BLAINE	P3382	1.25

Buy them at your local bookstores or use this handy coupon for ordering:

FAWCETT PUBLICATIONS, P.O. Box 1014, Greenwich Conn. 06830

Please send me the books I have checked above. Orders for less than 5 books must include 60c for the first book and 25c for each additional book to cover mailing and handling. Orders of 5 or more books postage is Free. I enclose $_____ in check or money order.

Mr/Mrs/Miss_____

Address_____

City_____ State/Zip_____

Please allow 4 to 5 weeks for delivery. This offer expires 6/78.　A-1